Suddenly, Bond was moving faster . . . beyond the speed of skiing. And below him was nothing . . .

His skis were flat against the snow. His heart was pounding. What was beyond the wide, leering mouth that stretched below him? He coiled himself like a spring. Then he was in the air, turning, turning, like a rag doll dropped from a window. He fought to reach his right arm behind his left shoulder, fumbling for a semicircle of metal on his haversack. There! He pulled and closed his eyes. Something behind him crackled like machine-gun fire, and he had a billowing glimpse of red, white and blue.

In the town of Chamonix, an old man shaded his eyes against the sun and looked up into the mountains. A man had just parachuted off the Aiguille du Mort. He could see the Union Jack emblem on the parachute. English!

Crazy English!

"THE SPY WHO LOVED ME"

A novel by
Christopher Wood

Based on the screenplay by
Christopher Wood &
Richard Maibaum

WARNER BOOKS

A Warner Communications Company

To Lewis Gilbert. Without whom . . .

WARNER BOOKS EDITION

Copyright © Glidrose Publications Ltd. as
Trustee 1977.
All rights reserved.

ISBN 0-446-84544-2

This Warner Books Edition is published by
arrangement with Glidrose Productions Ltd.

Warner Books, Inc., 75 Rockefeller Plaza, New York, N.Y. 10019

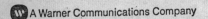 A Warner Communications Company

Printed in the United States of America

Not associated with Warner Press, Inc. of Anderson, Indiana

First Printing: June, 1977

10 9 8 7 6 5 4 3 2 1

Chapter 1

LOVE IN THE AFTERNOON

The girl lay back against the pillow and looked out on to the balcony. The man was still leaning against the balustrade, his hands spread wide and his head tilted forward as he examined something that was happening on the beach. He was naked except for a light-blue towel hitched around his waist. Although in repose, there was a quality of tension about him, like a baited trap. His body was not conspicuously muscled, but lean and hard. The girl knew that.

She pulled the sheet up about her own naked body and willed the man to turn round. He did not move. She turned and looked at the man's watch beside the bed. It was a Rolex Oyster Perpetual. The slim antennae hands showed four o'clock; an afternoon when the heat still clung persistently, sulkily refusing to give way to the inevitability of evening. The girl dabbed her cheek with the sheet and changed her position against the pillow. She wanted him to come back to her, but she was a proud girl and she did not want to ask. Nothing that she could think of saying sounded anything more than an attempt to make conversation. And conversation was a way of asking.

The girl looked down at the innocent swelling of her breasts beneath the sheet and blushed. Was it obvious? Could anybody tell at a glance that she had been making love—wild, beautiful love? She pulled her fingers through her hair trying to find how tangled it was. There had been a Greta Garbo film about a queen who was trapped in a wayside inn with a man. He did not know that she was a queen, and as the snow separated them from the outside world they had stayed in a room and made love. And the queen had wandered around the room touching the now familiar objects and consigning them to her memory. For she would never come back to this room and nothing with the man would ever be the same again.

What in this room was to be stored away? It was a sad room, the furniture heavy and ill-matched as so often in hotels, and the lining of the tall curtains beginning to drift away at the seams. No paintings hung on the heavy wood panelling, and the carpet was an unlovely gray.

A cry from the beach distracted her, and she looked out once more toward the man on the balcony. A shiver of wind, the first of the day, tugged at the curtains, and he turned and approached her. She gazed at the face as if seeing it for the first time. It was dark and clean-cut and the eyes were set wide and level under straight, rather long black brows. The longish straight nose ran down to a short upper lip below which was a wide and finely drawn mouth. The eyes were hard and the mouth was cruel, the line of the jaw was straight and firm.

The girl felt herself becoming hot and moist and was ashamed, because she was not a promiscuous girl. She lowered her gaze. The man took her chin in his hand and forced it up so that he could look into her eyes. "You know that I'm going this evening. I have a job to do."

She nodded. "You told me." Why was he telling her again? Was it his way of saying firmly that the pleasant interlude was over? Or was he in a way excusing himself? Apologizing for making love to her and then leaving her? Whatever it was, she wanted him to kiss her. To kiss her and press her back into the pillows and hold her tight and make her forget everything except the marvellous feeling that had spilled over her the last time.

The man leaned forward again. "You are the most beautiful woman I have ever seen." He looked into her eyes for several seconds and then abruptly kissed her with such passion that she expected to taste blood on her lips. His hard, blunt shoulders bore her down, and the sheet was contemptuously torn aside like a leaf from a calendar. The girl closed her eyes.

The jangle of the telephone was obscene. There were three lights in its base—red, yellow and green—and the red light was flashing. The man cursed, rolled to the edge of the bed, and snatched up the receiver. The voice on the other end of the line sounded very far away and was difficult to pick out through the static.

The girl watched the man's face as he talked, and her last hopes disappeared. Eventually, he held the receiver over the rest like a bomb waiting to be dropped.

"A change of plan?"

The man nodded glumly. "Apparently. You are to report to Moscow immediately."

The girl smiled a brief, sad smile of farewell and then swung her long legs from the bed. "Tell them that I am leaving immediately Sergei," she said.

Chapter 2

PISTE DANGEREUSE!

James Bond was angry with himself. He had committed a number of elementary blunders which a man of his training and experience should not have committed. He had been guilty of hubris and complacency. To put it in more direct terms, he had been a damn fool.

To start with, he should never have trusted the girl. Women you pick up in casinos are either straightforward whores or have run out of money playing some ridiculous system. Either way, they are going to be very expensive and probably very neurotic. Bond loved gambling because to him tension was a form of relaxation, but he should have been more wary of the lynx-eyed redhead spilling five-hundred-franc plaques around his ankles and receiving his offer of a drink with an alacrity considerably less discreet than the scent she was wearing—Fracas by Pinguet. Anybody knowing that he was in town would have expected him to make an appearance at the casino and could have organized the assignation accordingly. *Mea culpa.*

Bond was in Chamonix. M had suggested that he needed a few days' "holiday" and that the mountain air—a little skiing, a little walking—would do him good. In the summer you have to go high to ski. Through the Mont Blanc tunnel and up the Italian side of the Monte Bianco—somehow it did not seem to be the same mountain in Italian. Bond was not feeling charitable toward Italians. They had descended like a cloud of black *corbeaux* on the casino at Chamonix, wandering from table to table casting plaques upon the water and making too much noise. In an attempt to parlay large numbers of inflated lira into deflated francs they played everything badly and impeded Bond's concentration with their nudging badinage.

The girl said that she came to Chamonix every summer, though in winter she skied at Courchevel. Yes, the skiing at Tignes was excellent, but it was bleak and there were too many Germans. The Germans were not *sympathique*. She hoped Bond did not mind? Bond did not mind.

The girl also had a friend who worked for Heliski. He would be able to lift them high into the mountains by helicopter where they could find the best snow conditions. There were huts with bunks up there. They could spend the night.

It was when they were going up the face of the Aiguille du Mort that Bond first began to have doubts. The Aiguille du Mort drops sheer for two thousand feet, and even in the severest winter conditions, never more than a powdering of snow clings to the shallow contours of its bleak, granite face. But it was not the physical danger that Bond feared. He was aware of the isolation toward which he was heading. Over the lip of the peak and it was a lunar landscape clad in unending snow. The neat pattern of Chamonix disappearing below him was a child's toytown. Above his head, the rotor droned and his breath froze against the reinforced window of the cabin. The wind was streaming the snow off the peaks like smoke, and the Gyrafrance lurched in the treacherous air currents. Outside the cabin the refracted image of the pilot peered back at him as if projected against the cliff face—butterfly-wing mirror sunglasses slanting away beside the nose, a brutal smudge of a mustache. The man had hardly touched his hand when they greeted each other. It was as if Bond was something not to be touched, something that was to be moved quickly from one place to the other and then dropped.

The helicopter hit an air pocket and fell ten feet. Bond felt his stomach tighten like a fist. He looked toward the girl. She looked tense, and he could see the whites of her knuckles as she gripped the pilot's frameback seat. Was it just the flight?

"When are we going to go down?"

"Soon, darleeng. The snow will be good. Wait and see."

Do I have an alternative? thought Bond. He wished he could feel his Walther PPK 7.65mm nestling inside his trouser band. But like a damn fool he had left it behind, hidden in the recess behind the hideous cuckoo clock that guarded the exterior of his room in the Hotel Dahu.

Bond tapped the glass of his Rod 88 goggles and examined the girl more closely. She had, he supposed, a typically French face. A dark gypsy sluttishness tamed into sophistication. Her green almond eyes seldom seemed to be more than half open and sheltered between a foliage of long untidy lashes which looked as if she had just washed them and found them impossible to manage. Her nose was short and tilted up at the end and her lips thrust out, permanently pert and premeditated as if she was just about to blow a kiss. Her hair, now tucked under a close-fitting, knitted woollen cap, was cut casually to fall across her forehead and hang in inverted question marks about her shoulders.

"Why do you bring this?" She pointed to the small red haversack that Bond had taken from his shoulders when he climbed into the Gyrafrance.

"It's my mountain survival kit."

"There is everything we need to survive in the 'ut. You will see."

"I was brought up never to take chances." Was it his imagination or did the pilot's mouth tighten into a faint smile?

Now they were over the lip of the Aiguille, and the turbulence ceased. Chamonix had disappeared, but at least he was spared that nerve-fraying view down the cliff face.

"*On va descendre tout suite,*" said the pilot without turning his head. "Two minute," he repeated, presumably for Bond's benefit, and jerked a thumb toward the snow.

The helicopter skimmed over a ridge, and Bond looked down on a wide, undulating expanse of snow broken by occasional rock formations. Far, far to his right was the line of squat *télécabines*, etched against the sky like a string of pack ponies, that made their way from the Aiguille du Midi to the Italian side of the frontier. To the far left of his vision must be the Swiss frontier. Three countries interlocking in a vast white wilderness. It must be easy to move from one to the other if you knew the mountains. What country were they in now? The helicopter came down to hover above the snow, the blades stirring up a blizzard. The pilot said something to the girl which Bond did not catch, because of the noise, and pushed back the hatch cover. The rush of cold air stung Bond's cheek.

"I take it we're being left here?" shouted Bond.

The girl nodded and gestured toward the settling snow. This was not deep powder but layers of snow beaten down by successive falls. At this altitude there were probably frequent snowfalls even in the middle of summer. It was early enough in the day for the surface still to be frozen and the helicopter skis had pressed out their shape to the depth of a couple of inches. Bond took a deep breath and felt his lungs protest. At thirteen thousand feet the lack of oxygen can have a fit man wondering why he is suddenly breathing like a grampus.

Bond kept a wary eye on the pilot and indicated with a courteous extension of the hand that the girl should descend first. He did not want to step in the snow, receive a bullet in the stomach, and live just long enough to see the helicopter spiralling away into the sun. To his relief the girl acknowledged the gesture with a smile and swung her legs out of the cabin. He dropped down beside her and

11

removed his Rossignol ST Competition skis from the out-side of the Gyrafrance. The pilot was looking back impatiently as if eager to be off.

"Is he picking us up?"

"No. We will ski down." The girl took her skis and moved away from the helicopter. Bond pulled on his gloves, adjusted his goggles against the glare, and followed her.

"Why are you looking at me?" said the girl.

"I was just thinking how pretty you were," said Bond, examining the outline of her suit for any sign of a concealed weapon.

The girl was called Martine Blanchaud and had said that she lived in Lyons where her father owned a business. She had been unhappily married and stayed with friends when she came to Chamonix. Bond had never seen any of the friends. She was always alone when he had seen her at the casino.

The helicopter sprayed up more snow and then slid away over the ridge. Bond felt a sense of challenge and excitement unrelated to his possible predicament. The mountains about him set the pulse racing. Peaks sharpened as if with a knife falling behind each other in a march to a perfect eggshell-blue sky; a view which embraced three countries and probably extended to a hundred miles. The vapor trail of an airplane cut a line through the sky, and hundreds of feet below, a hawk plucked at the wind with its wings, hovered, and then glided out of sight.

"Do you not want to ski?"

"I was looking at the mountains," said Bond.

The girl rested her hand lightly on his shoulder so that she could brush the snow from her boot. "When you see them all the time, you get used to them."

"Perhaps." Bond felt a sense of unreality. He had been dropped onto the roof of the world and he had done nothing to earn these spirit-enriching vistas the reward of those who had bravely scaled up the face of a mountain. Bond preferred his pleasures hard-won. He stamped hard into his skis, hunched his shoulders, and stabbed at the snow with his sticks. Some expiation was clearly necessary.

"You 'ave old-fashioned *batons*," said the girl. "You should get the new ones. See 'ow they curve around be'ind your back when you schuss? There is less wind resistance."

Bond looked at the girl's sticks, which looked like alloy pigs' tails. He shook his head. "They're not going to make any difference to my skiing. I'll stick to these, thanks."

The girl shrugged and poked at one of her ski bindings. "Follow me. There are some crevasses here." Are there indeed, thought Bond. A man can lie for a long time in the bottom of a crevasse. He cursed himself again for his folly.

The girl started to ski, carving out a zigzag pattern in the deep snow. She skied very upright, like most women, but she was graceful and had perfect balance. Bond watched her with grudging admiration. As a rule he admired women practicing any sport as much as Dr. Johnson admired them preaching, but he made an exception in the cases of fencing and skiing. These were two pursuits that could enhance their femininity rather than grotesquely diminish it.

Bond tightened the clasps on his haversack and felt the steel frame bite into his shoulderblades. There was a touch of condensation in his goggles and he pulled them away from his face a couple of times and adjusted the visor to clear the mist. The leather-buckled straps of his Kerma Zicral sticks sat lightly on the tops of his hands and as a gust of wind cuffed snow into the air, he shifted his weight and sent the two-meter Rossignol STs sliding down the slope.

As always with any sport not constantly practiced, there was a moment of doubt. Would the skill return when summoned? As he gathered speed and prepared for the first turn, Bond told himself to relax. No one skis well when he is tensed. Ahead, the wide expanse of snow lay unbroken save for the graceful tracery of the girl's track. Bond's skis rattled and he moved them an extra inch apart before picking his spot with his stick. His body rose and he pressed down hard, carving the pattern of the turn with his knees. The skis hissed through the snow and Bond felt himself secure in the perfect arc of movement that

13

makes a good turn. He sank down and then rose again effortlessly into the next. A glance behind told him that it was better than the first, more crisply etched and with less powder thrown out at the edge. Satisfied, Bond skied fast to where the girl was waiting.

She looked at him admiringly. "You are a very good skier." There was a slight note of surprise in her voice.

"I try," said Bond.

They skied for another hour before they came to the chalet refuge. Bond had kept careful watch but had seen no sign that there was anyone in this part of the mountains but themselves. He had noticed chamois tracks, but that was all. Perhaps his instinct had been wrong, for once. The helicopter pilot had been disgruntled because he was having problems with his wife or mistress—or both—and Martine Blanchaud was like himself, merely looking for congenial company and not part of some sinister plot. Maybe M's surmise that he was run down and needed a few days' holiday had been correct. M's surmises usually were.

The hut was of typical alpine construction—wide and low and backed into the mountain as if prepared to sell its life dearly against any avalanche that rolled down from above. The logs from which it was made criss-crossed and stuck out at two corners and the tiny windows were sunk back in the walls like an old man's eyes. Six feet of snow on the roof gave it the appearance of some exotic gâteau.

Bond was glad to see that the snow around the door was undisturbed. He took off his skis and tried the door. At first he thought it was locked, but it was merely frozen. He put his shoulder against it and it gave with a sound like a pistol shot. Some snow fell on his head, and the girl laughed. "Careful," said Bond. "I might put you across my knee."

The girl raised an intrigued eyebrow, and Bond wondered if she understood the exact meaning of the expression. She was very pretty, and the morning's skiing had rekindled a number of his appetites. Perhaps it had been the Italians and the losing streak at the casino that had made him liverish.

14

As was his habit when playing roulette, Bond had borrowed the chef's card and studied the run of the ball since the session opened at three o'clock. He knew that mathematically it meant nothing, but it was his convention to take careful note of any peculiarities in the run of the wheel and to act upon them. In this instance the card had told him nothing of interest except that five of the last six numbers to come up had been lower than twenty-five. It was Bond's practice to play always with the wheel and only start on a new tack when zero came up. On this night he had decided to follow the wheel and back the first two dozens. The dozens pay odds of two to one, which meant that for every thousand francs Bond bet he would make a profit of five hundred francs provided that neither zero nor a number higher than twenty-four came up.

On the first throw, the ivory ball had dropped into the twenty-five. The second throw was thirty-two. Bond had made no sign but merely marked his card. The third throw was another twenty-five. Bond had stayed with the first two dozens and increased his stake to the maximum.

As he did every time, the croupier had picked up the ball with his right hand, given one of the four spokes of the wheel a controlled clockwise twist with the same hand, and flicked the ball around the outer rim of the wheel anticlockwise against the spin. The ball had run smoothly at first and then jiggled and joggled happily over the slots as the wheel began to lose momentum. Its carefree progress contrasted with the drawn faces around the table, some of them trying to keep pace with its movement like spectators at a tennis match.

"Zero!" Had there been a hint of triumph in that cry? Nobody had been on zero, and the table had been cleared in favor of the bank.

So opened one of the least successful gaming sessions Bond had ever known. He had limped away from the tables with Martine Blanchaud in exchange for a total loss of eight thousand francs. Perhaps now was the moment to discover if Mademoiselle Blanchaud could provide adequate recompense for such a loss.

15

The inside of the hut was sparsely furnished with a few solid wooden chairs and a hewn table. There was a large wood-framed fireplace with a fire laid and waiting to be lit, and a two-tier bunk bed, each compartment being of strictly single dimensions. Particles of dust hung in the descending shaft of sunlight that penetrated one of the small, thick-paned windows, and there was a thick coating of dust on most surfaces. Two tall doors flanked the fireplace and were presumably cupboards.

"It needs a little money spent on it," said Bond. "Kind of someone to leave us a fire."

"Tu as du feu?"

Bond proffered his battered Ronson and enjoyed the line of the girl's behind as she sat on her haunches to light the fire. Nobody has yet managed to design a ski outfit that enhances the work God put into the female body, but this concealed less than most.

There was a crackle, a flame, a thin, determined column of smoke, and then the fire began to draw lustily. The girl rose to him triumphantly. *"Voilà!"*

"Do they have Girl Guides in France?"

Again the look of puzzlement. "You mean, on the mountains?"

Bond took the girl into his arms and felt her warm, soft breasts against his chest. Soon he would kiss her and make them hard.

"No," he said. "I mean something completely different. Girl Guides are—" He broke off, staring through the fragment of window not obscured by drifts. He was looking at a perfect field of snow traversed by distant ski tracks weaving down the side of the mountain. Three pairs of ski tracks. Bond's heart raced. The tracks had not been there when they came. Somebody was coming toward the hut.

Bond pushed the girl away and immediately saw fear in her eyes. She knew. What the hell was he going to do? Certainly not stay here. He looked into the frightened, betraying eyes and threw his arm roughly around the girl's waist. He snatched her to him so that her lips trembled an inch from his.

16

"Might as well find out what you taste like!" He kissed her hard and cruelly and hurled her back across the room so that she sprawled dangerously close to the fire she had just lit. Turning his back contemptuously, he stooped to gaze through the window. The path of the ski tracks was obscured by an outcropping of rock in the foreground. For two hundred yards in front of him there was no sign of movement. The men must be in the hollow behind the rock. He could imagine them briskly side-stepping up the slope, the locomotive spurts of breath escaping from their lips. He turned toward the girl, who was still squatting near the fireplace watching him warily. Get going!

He had taken two steps toward the door when an impulse made him spin around and examine the two cupboards. The first yielded nothing of interest—two folded *duvets*, tins of *cassoulet*, and candles.

The second was locked.

Bond took his knee to it and then followed through with the whole weight of his foot encased in its Handson ski boot. Splinters of wood burst from the area of the lock, and the door crashed open. What Bond saw made him want to be sick. A pretty girl in a transparent laundry bag. Naked. Dead. Her hands tied behind her back. Her body mutilated. Disgusting smears of blood on the thick polythene. Her flesh bruised and swollen.

Bond spun around toward Martine Blanchaud. The expression of stupefied horror on her face saved her life. This was one turn of the wheel she had not known about.

Bond clattered clumsily across the room and threw open the door. The midday sun was strong enough to start the icicles dripping, and a ragged trench mark followed the line of the eaves. Bond snatched his skis, which were propped up against the wall, and threw them down in the snow. Damn! There was ice on one of his boots. He tried to force it into the binding and then hacked savagely with the tip of his stick. The black, hard rime fell away parsimoniously as if being sculpted. The men must be near now. Bond scraped again and drove his foot down savagely.

17

Click!

It was not the sound of the binding gripping but of a carbine being cocked. Bond ducked instinctively, and the shot sprayed him with splinters of wood from the spot where his head had been. One ski was now secure, and Bond kicked the other forward and hopped after it so that he did not present a sitting target. He glided on one ski and, catching up with the second, brought his foot down until it made contact with the binding. A second bullet kicked up snow a couple of feet behind him. Bond felt the desperate electricity of fear circuiting his body. If he could not get his boot in the binding . . . Bending forward with his weight agonizingly poised on his right knee, Bond steadied the errant ski and slid the toe of his boot under the expanded C of metal that manipulated the front release mechanism. His heel wavered and then steadied momentarily between the sprung platform of the back restraint. He sucked in his breath and presssed down. The automatic stop resisted and then clicked down. The boot was held.

Bond skate-skied behind a pile of logs buried by the snow and surveyed the open ground before him. There were two men on skis wearing white military-type one-piece suits with hoods. They were both armed with carbines, and one of the men was kneeling to take up a better firing position. Even as he ducked back behind the logs a bullet screamed into them, kicking up a flurry of snow. Bond jump-turned and headed for the slope, running at a reverse angle to the one by which he and the girl had reached the hut. He drove his skis against the snow as if they were ice skates and dropped to the schuss position as soon as he began to pick up speed. That way he made a smaller target and moved faster. There was a pause in which he could hear his heart beating and then another shot that whistled over his right shoulder. He rose just long enough to turn and then took the steepest line.

Within a second he knew that he had made a mistake.

The shot that sang off his boot buckles had come from below him. The first two men had been beaters driving him toward the third. They must have realized that there was a good chance of them being seen approaching the hut, and had laid their plans accordingly. Once again he, James Bond, had been found wanting. He was skiing into a trap.

He could see the third man now, fifty yards below him and to the right. The man was holding his rifle but not bothering to take aim. He was waiting to see what Bond did. Whether he stopped or came into closer range.

Bond glanced behind him. There was no sign of the other men over the brow of the slope. Below, steep crags rose up on both sides, funnelling him toward a narrow, precipitous corridor. It was this that the third man was guarding. A cold sweat prickled Bond's armpits. Think fast, damn you! You got yourself into this, now get yourself out. The soft life has caught up with you, Bond. The next comfortable, plush-lined *boîte* you find yourself in will not be a *boîte de nuit* but a *boîte de la longue nuit*—a coffin.

Bond stopped in a flurry of snow and slid his right hand from beneath the restraining strap of his stick. Holding it freely and, like its fellow, away from his body, he skied slowly toward the man trying to look as innocuous as possible.

Immediately, the man half raised his rifle and then lowered it. Clearly, he was puzzled. Was Bond giving himself up? Should he shoot or should he wait?

"Qu'est-ce qui arrive?" shouted Bond. *"C'est une zone limitée?"* He was thirty yards from the man and could make out his cold, hard, death's-head features. The rifle swung up. The man had decided to kill.

Bond raised the stick in his right hand in a gesture that must have seemed like admonishment. His fingers fumbled and twisted at the point where the zicral shaft met the grip. Something gave, and Bond could feel pressure against the glove-clad pad of his thumb. The barrel of the machine carbine was on a direct line for his heart and the man's shoulder hunched forward. Bond squeezed the metal nerve with a desperation born of fear. There was a violent yellow

19

flash and a pall of blood and guts was thrown twenty feet behind the man with a noise like a whip-crack. Through the smoking end of his now pointless ski stick Bond watched the rifle drop, the hands involuntarily fall to the obscene, pumping hole, the look of unbelieving amazement on the face, the ghastly recognition, the two steps back taken in death, and the final collapse into the bloody shroud of snow. It was over in seconds, but Bond knew that the memory of that death would stay with him for the rest of his life.

Another shot came from behind, no better directed than the rest. Farewell to obsequies. Bond dropped to his now familiar crouch and skated for the corridor between the rocks. Sufficient momentum attained, he dropped to the eggshell position and hugged his knees.

Behind him, the eyes of the two men were not for their stricken comrade but for the departing Bond. One of them quickly snapped into firing position and spun around angrily as his comrade knocked aside the barrel of his rifle. The second man smiled and nodded toward the corridor. "Aiguille du Mort."

Bond was moving faster than he knew how to ski. The descent was precipitous, and below him was a sheer edge. His skis were flat against the snow and slapping like a motorboat travelling at high speed across a choppy sea. His heart was pounding, and the mounting acceleration of his stone-like fall threatened to tear the goggles from his face. What was beyond the wide, leering mouth that stretched below him? In five seconds he would know, if he did not catch an edge and catapult himself against the jagged rocks that menaced the narrow corridor. He coiled himself like a spring and then—and then—nothing. The snow disappeared from beneath his feet and he was launched into space. Thousands of feet below him a crisscross of man-made lines—the town of Chamonix. He had skied off the edge of the Aiguille du Mort.

Bond began to turn in the air like a rag doll dropped from a window. The force of descent ripped a ski from his boot and he felt a sharp pain in his knee as it was

20

twisted savagely by the motion. His widespread arms clawed at the air trying to achieve some balance, but the world spun past—granite, sky, snow. The wind screamed. It had been like this in dreams. The sudden jolt and the falling, falling, falling. But in dreams you woke up before you spattered against the rocks like a bird's dropping. Bond fought to reach his right arm behind his left shoulder. The second ski had gone and there was now some pattern to his descent. His fingers closed against the edge of the haversack and then lost contact. It seemed that he had been kicking in space for minutes. He clamped his hand to his shoulder and fumbled desperately. This time his fingers felt something. A semicircle of metal. He pulled and closed his eyes.

Suddenly something behind him crackled like machine-gun fire and there was a billowing glimpse of red, white, and blue. A giant hand seized him by the scruff of the neck and pulled the world into focus. His speed of descent slackened magically and suddenly he could see his boots dangling below him. He had time to breathe, to look up at the bulging panels of silk above his head, to realize that he was alive.

In the town of Chamonix an old man shaded his eyes against the sun and looked up into the mountains. A man had just parachuted off the Aiguille du Mort. He must be an Englishman because it was possible to see the reverse side of the Union Jack emblem on his parachute and because only an Englishman would do a thing like that. "*Ils sont fous, les anglais*," he said, not without a trace of grudging admiration, and hurried on down the Avenue du Bouchet.

Nearly nine thousand feet above the town, Sergei Borzov of SMERSH Otdyel II, the Operations and Executions branch of the murder apparat of the Russian K.G.B., lay with his mouth open and watched his blood melting a hole in the snow. It would not be melting it for much longer. Already a long shadow was falling across the slope and the cold reached out ahead of it. He would never see her again, or the hotel on the Black Sea, or the

21

children playing on the beach. All that he had consigned to memory before turning and funnelling his soul into her eyes. The room had been cool and dark and deep like a grave. The curtains stirring in a dying wind. The sheet about her breasts white as snow. White as snow.

The black shadow passed over the man and he closed his eyes and died.

Chapter 3

DEATH TO SPIES

Anya Amasova felt uneasy as the nondescript ZIS saloon approached the familiar drabness of the Sretenka Ulitsa. Why did they want her at such short notice? Why had no reasons been given? What had she done wrong? The last was the most persistent and worrying consideration. Nobody who worked for the K.G.B. or any other branch of the Soviet bureaucracy could afford to feel beyond blame. Original sin was as much a tenet of the Communist faith as of the Christian. Perhaps they had found out about her affair with Sergei—she interrupted her train of thought to scold herself. Not affair—that was one of their words. Cheap and shoddy. Transitory. She must find a better way to describe what had happened. Perhaps they had found out that she and Sergei had fallen in love. The room was almost certainly bugged, and there might even have been a concealed camera. Such things were not unknown.

But could they object to her falling in love? Yes, they could object to anything. The state was your only lover and the penalties for unfaithfulness were severe.

"Comrade Major." The driver had turned around and was looking at her with deadpan eyes. They had arrived. Number 13 Sretenka Ulitsa, headquarters of SMERSH.

Anya glanced up and caught a glimpse of her eyes in the driver's mirror. It is at such offguard moments that you really see yourself, and Anya was disturbed by the look of fear in her eyes. The open, vulnerable wariness. Not for the first time, she wondered if she was cut out for the work the state had chosen for her. Perhaps her superiors at Otdyel 4 had come to the same conclusion.

SMERSH is a contraction of *Smiert Spionam*, which means "Death to Spies". The organization currently employs a total of 60,000 men, women, and transvestites, although the number changes continually as a result of operational losses and the elimination of weak and unreliable elements.

Anya Amasova's progress within Otdyel 4 of SMERSH— the section responsible for internal security in the armed forces—had been steady rather than spectacular. She had been the youngest of four children born to the wife of a country doctor. After his death in a car accident, Anya's mother had been grateful for the suggestion from the headmistress of the local school that Anya was a bright girl who might qualify for training at a special "Technical College" near Leningrad. Anya had passed the examination with flying colors and was soon attending classes in "General Political Knowledge" and "Tactics, Agitation, and Propaganda." In her third year she moved on to "Technical Subjects" and became proficient in the use of codes and ciphers. She was marked "satisfactory" in Communications and became conversant with the intricacies of Contacts, Cut-outs, Couriers and Post Boxes. Her Fieldwork was also deemed satisfactory. In tests she received high marks for Vigilance, Presence of Mind, Courage, and Coolness. Her mark for Discretion was average.

After Leningrad came the School for Terror and Diversion at Kuchino, outside Moscow. Anya's marks in judo and athletics were high and she became a capable wireless operator and excellent photographer. She also had her first lover, her small-arms instructor, who was runner-up in the Soviet Rifle Championships. Anya became an excellent pistol shot.

Up to now, all her training had been in the Soviet Union, but with the termination of her course at S.T.D. she was sent to work at an Avanpost in Czechoslovakia. These mobile operation groups were engaged in surveying and, where necessary, liquidating Russian spies and party workers in the satellite countries. Anya's work in this sector had been beyond reproach, although it was noted on her *zapiska* that she had always delegated the act of execution.

Upon recall to Moscow, Anya had been given the rank of Major and assigned to Military Records, where she was granted access to the files on all military personnel below the rank of General or its equivalent. In conjunction with other departments of SMERSH she was responsible for the vital character assessment that preceded any promotion or demotion. She had written copious and highly detailed reports, and as a result of her conscientiousness—although she was unaware of it—three men and a woman had been hanged with fine wire. A death for traitors that Stalin had borrowed from Hitler.

The bizarre course from which she had just been summoned was one that united several branches of the ever-expanding octopus of SMERSH, and it was here that she had met Sergei Borzov for the first time. He had been reticent about his role in the organization, as had she. It was never wise to talk too much, and dangerous to ask questions.

One of the two sentries outside Number 13 bent down to open the door and his sub-machine gun banged against it clumsily. The driver protested about his paintwork and then stopped abruptly when the sentry looked at him. Anybody involved with SMERSH was to be feared. Anya left the car and walked up the broad flight of steps leading to the big iron double door. She continued to feel uneasy.

At first glance the large olive-green room on the second floor could have been mistaken for a government office

25

anywhere in the world. The floor was fitted with finest-quality carpet, and a large oak desk dominated one end of the room. Two spacious windows gave onto a courtyard at the back of the building and were fringed by heavy brocade curtains. On one wall was a large portrait of Brezhnev surrounded by a thin border of faded wallpaper which indicated where an even larger portrait of Stalin had once hung.

On the desk were two wire-frame baskets marked IN and OUT, a heavy glass ashtray, a carafe of water and tumblers, and four telephones. One of the telephones was marked in white with the letters V.Ch. These letters stood for *Vysoko-Chastoty*, or High Frequency. Only fifty supreme officials were connected to the V.Ch. switchboard, and all were Ministers of state or heads of selected departments. It was served by a small exchange in the Kremlin operated by professional security officers. They could not overhear conversations on it, but every word spoken over its lines was automatically recorded. It was this telephone that had summoned Major Anya Amasova.

"Ah, Major Amasova! Come and sit down." The warmth in the man's voice surprised Anya. She had only met him on three occasions when answering questions about reports she had submitted.

Colonel-General Nikitin, the Head of SMERSH, was standing behind his desk and extending a hand toward a straight-backed red leather chair. He was a tall man dressed in a crisply pressed khaki tunic with a high collar and dark blue cavalry trousers with two thin red stripes down the side. The trousers disappeared into riding boots of black, highly polished leather. On the breast of the tunic were three rows of medal ribbons—two Orders of Lenin, Order of Alexander Nevsky, Order of the Red Banner, two Orders of the Red Star, the Twenty Years' Service Medal, and a ribbon that Anya did not recognize. It must belong to the newly struck Sino-Soviet Friendship Medal. Anya memorized the colors so that she could look it up when she got back to Military Records. Above the rows of ribbons hung the gold star of a Hero of the Soviet Union.

"I apologize for my late appearance, Comrade General. You heard of the technical problems with the Ilyushin?"

Nikitin held up a peremptory hand that told her that her question was unnecessary. "I was informed." He paused and looked hard into her face. "How was the course?"

Anya was thrown by the suddenness of the question. It redoubled her fears that she had been summoned because of her relationship with Sergei. She could feel herself blushing. For the first time, she wondered if his mission might have been engineered to separate them.

"Very interesting, Comrade General."

"*Very* interesting?" General Nikitin smiled. His face was rough and calloused like a potato left to dry in the sun, but the eyes could have been prised from a week-old corpse. There was no visible sign of life behind them.

Anya felt her blush deepen. "It was a most unusual and unexpected assignment."

"Which you took the fullest advantage of."

Somewhere, in a distant corner of the room, a bluebottle was beating against a window pane. A furious, high-pitched buzz and then silence for ten seconds, then the buzzing starting again. Nikitin was still probing her with his cold, lusterless eyes.

"The scope of the course came as a surprise to me." This was if anything an understatement. The movement order assigning her to the dacha on the southeastern coast of the Crimea had confined itself to the words "Cold War Techniques." It had come as considerably more than a surprise on the first morning of the course, in the company of twenty attractive young men and women, to be confronted by a folder with *Sex as a Weapon* printed in bold letters on its shiny cover. What followed had been a revelation. Lectures, films, demonstrations, what was discreetly described as "Controlled Participation" with electrodes attached to various parts of the body to measure the degree of response; tests, more measurements, interviews, instruction in the latest cosmetics available in the West and how to apply them; a course in *haute couture*. Mili-

27

tary Records had suddenly seemed like a different world. Anya's final rating had been "E Sensual," which she knew meant that she made love well and enjoyed it. Despite every laboratory test that the scientists could devise, her emotional stability had remained an unknown quantity. The private report which she did not see said that she had exceptional potential but with an element of risk attached to it.

And in the middle of all this she had fallen in love. It must have been that to which Colonel-General Nikitin had been referring with his talk of taking the fullest advantage. Suddenly she felt a rush of anger. What right did they have to tell her whether she could love or not? Was she to be punished because amongst all the guile and artifice, the antiseptic passion and the throbbing wires she had found something that could never be contained in any tawdry manual of eroticism? She stared back into Nikitin's soulless eyes with a new determination.

The Colonel-General nodded as if in agreement with some sentiment that needed no expression. "He was a fine young man. One of our best operatives." He studied her wondering face. "Such a thing as you had could not escape notice. There is no need of films and tape recordings."

But they are very useful, thought Anya. What did he mean—"was"?

"And up to now, conspicuously efficient. It just shows how these affairs of the heart can affect people."

"What do you mean?" Anya saw the pinpoint of red behind the eyes and corrected herself." What do you mean, Comrade General?"

Nikitin reached into a drawer and produced a small, rectangular scrap of paper. A light was extinguished before he opened his mouth. "I very much regret to inform you that Comrade Sergei Borzov was killed on active service behind enemy lines. I have just heard the news." He listened to the girl's sobs, then dropped his hand to switch off the tape recorder below the desk.

With unusual haste, the general levered himself from his chair and circumvented the desk. "You must not blame yourself too much, my dear. Others might read more into the whole business than it warrants, but you can rely upon me to keep an open mind. If Sergei's judgment was at fault, it was not because of you—because of your—your affair." The General seemed pleased at having found the word. "You are young and very beautiful, and you have need of guidance—of protection. You need a friend who is well placed. Especially at the moment." The rough hand dropped to her knee like a paw.

"Where did he die?"

"In the French Alps. He was on a mission to eliminate a British agent. He failed." With the recorder turned off, Nikitin was letting the words tumble out. His eyes had found light from somewhere and they glistened as he watched his hand push up her skirt like a burrowing animal.

Anya felt her nostrils twitch before the scent of roses that some Russian men wear to disguise the fact that they cannot be bothered to wash. Nikitin's head was bending toward her lap, and she saw that the crimped line across his forehead denoted a wig. An obscene dribble of rust-colored adhesive leaked from beneath the hairline.

Anya fought a desire to vomit. Her skirt was now pressed back against her waist, and the animal hand . . . She rose to her feet and thrust Nikitin aside as she launched herself at the desk. She pressed a finger to her lips and snatched up a thin State-Issue ballpoint. Nikitin watched her like an animal ready to spring.

The record of Sergei's death still lay on the desk, and Anya turned it over and wrote urgently. This had to work. She had seen Nikitin's hand drop below the desk and she knew what it meant.

She finished her message and thrust it into Nikitin's wary hand. He looked at her with slow-burning hate and raised it to his eyes. "Most honored. But I know from Military Records that there is another microphone hidden in your room."

Nikitin raised his eyes from the message and for a second let them rest on the ceiling. Then he slowly made his way back around the table. He lowered himself into his chair, and a slight subsidence of the right shoulder revealed that a hand had been dropped. The eyes that looked toward Anya were as devoid of expression as the face of the moon.

"But I did not bring you here to discuss the unfortunate death of Comrade Borzov. There is an assignment of great importance for which I think you may be suited . . ."

Chapter 4

HUNT THE SUBMARINE

August had committed an act of treachery against the
English summer, and rain was lashing the windows of M's
office overlooking Regents Park.

The old man was having trouble with his pipe as usual.
Bond let him get on with it and gazed around at the
familiar fittings he had come to know so well over the
years. The venetian blinds that gave an impression of coolness even on the hottest day; the dark green Wilton carpet
leading to the big, red leather-topped desk; the twin-bladed
tropical fan, now immobile, set in the ceiling directly
above M's desk.

The Head of Britain's Secret Service had lost no time
in summoning Bond to his office. No sooner had Station J
contacted him at Chamonix and told him that his presence
was urgently required at headquarters than he had
screamed down the motorway to Geneva and caught the
first plane to London. And no sooner was he behind his
desk staring glumly at the pile of routine messages and
reports marked "for your urgent attention" that always

arrived in droves when he left the country than the telephone had rung.

"007."

"Can you come up?" It was the Chief of Staff.

"M?"

"Yes."

"What's it all about?"

"I don't know, but it's serious."

It always is, thought Bond as he put down the receiver. He left his office and took the elevator up to the top floor. The walk down the long, quiet corridor was familiar, and he knew exactly how many paces it would take. Thirty, before he came to the outer door of M's office. The girl behind the desk was unfamiliar and unbeautiful, so the smile that Bond bestowed upon her was dutiful rather than anticipatory. She bent forward and pressed the switch of the intercom.

"007 is here, sir."

"Send him in," said the metallic voice, and the red light which meant "On no account must I be disturbed" glowed above the door.

That had been ten minutes ago and Bond was still listening to the rasping and sucking noises. At last they stopped, and M dropped the still smoking stick of a match in the big copper ashtray.

"So you found Q's gadgets useful, did you, James?"

"Very efficacious, sir."

"I thought you were going to fire them into the side of mountains. That sort of thing."

"That was my intention, sir."

M attacked his pipe with a small pick and turned away to breathe clouds of smoke toward the ceiling. There was a dry twinkle in his eye as he turned back toward Bond. "Q will be very impressed when you submit your report. I don't think he had any idea that you were going to be so zealous in your testing of his new toys."

"It came as a surprise to me, sir."

M looked at Bond, not without affection. "While we're on the subject. We had a signal from the French D.S.T."

"What are they going to do?"

"Nothing." M registered the sharp rise of Bond's right eyebrow and continued. "They're leaving the matter in the hands of the local gendarmerie. A chalet fire of this description is not uncommon." Bond was now sitting forward in his chair. "Perhaps you did not notice that there was petrol stored by the hut—for the Snowcats. The young people must have tried to start a fire and—well, you know how dangerous it can be with petrol."

"A man and a girl." Bond nodded. A sensible way for them to have covered their traces. The man he had shot and the girl in the cupboard consigned to flames.

"There appear to have been two women and one man," said M. "The bodies burned almost beyond recognition. Any identification will have to wait for the next of kin to come forward."

Which could take a long, long time, thought Bond. So, Martine Blanchaud, or whatever her real name was, had paid the ultimate price for incompetence. There was only one organization capable of that combination of brutality, guile, and casual disregard for human life. Bond decided to express his feelings to M.

"I think it was SMERSH, sir. They were after me. But, like last time, they wanted to make me stink even before I was rotting in my coffin. There was a dead girl in the hut— some drugged little tart from the back streets of Lyons, most probably. They'd hacked her up like shark bait."

"And you were the shark." M nodded grimly. He could see the newspaper headlines ("Drug-Crazed British Agent Slays in Mountain Love Nest"), the Home Secretary on the telephone, the official denials, the snide questions from the fellow-travellers in the House of Commons, the satisfied smiles around the table of the High Presidium in the Kremlin. Yes, once again 007 had been fortunate. Was it Napoleon who had always supported one of his marshals because he was lucky? "Strange that this should happen now, James."

Bond looked at M inquiringly and reached for the flat, light gunmetal case containing fifty Balkan and Turkish mixture cigarettes, specially made for him by Morlands of Grosvenor Street. He extracted one and ran a finger over

33

the triple gold band before placing it between his lips. "What's up, sir?"

M's tranquil, lined sailor's face suddenly became tense. "What does H.M.S. *Ranger* mean to you, James?"

Bond flicked through the card index in his mind. "One of our Resolution class nuclear-powered ballistic missile submarines, sir." M's approving silence told him to continue. "Laid down by Vickers-Armstrong at Barrow-in-Furnace in 1967. Operational in 1971. Length approximately three hundred and seventy feet. Beam thirty-three feet. Surface displacement seven thousand five hundred tons—submerged eight thousand four hundred. Speed reputed to be twenty knots on the surface and twenty-five submerged—although the submerged figure may be on the slow side. Ship's complement, a hundred and forty-one men; nineteen officers and one hundred and thirty-five ratings—they operate on a two-crew basis to get maximum time at sea." Bond broke off and put the battered, oxidized Ronson to work on his cigarette. M's demanding eyes bored into him as he directed a thin stream of smoke toward the ceiling.

"And the armament?"

"Six conventional 533mm torpedo homing tubes placed forward and sixteen Polaris surface-to-surface intercontinental missiles with a range in excess of two thousand five hundred miles."

M continued to stare levelly. Bond noticed that his pipe had gone out. "H.M.S. *Ranger* has disappeared."

The rain persisted in its attack on the windows, and for long seconds its angry patter was the only sound heard in the cool, dark room.

"You mean, there's been an accident?"

M shook his head. "We don't know. Radio contact is intermittent. The Admiralty first became alarmed when there was no Sitrep from their last reporting point."

"They sail on a predetermined course?"

"Yes."

"So that if something had gone wrong and wireless communication had failed, they could be lying on the bottom anywhere over a distance of, say, two thousand miles?"

"Correct."

So why is the department being involved? thought Bond. We have no expertise in raising nuclear submarines from the bottom of the ocean. Especially if we have no idea where they are. He looked at M, expecting more.

"We don't necessarily believe that it's a question of mechanical failure. We have enjoyed the full cooperation of the United States Navy, whose tactical experience in this kind of situation is second to none, and we have found no trace of the *Ranger*."

"Are you suggesting that she's been destroyed by enemy action, sir?"

The lines on M's face suddenly seemed to be etched deeper. "Come here, James. I want you to look at something that arrived in the diplomatic bag from Cairo."

M produced a scuffed leather map case and drew out a cylinder of tightly rolled, translucent parchment. Bond moved to his side and looked down at the surface of the desk that had been specially prepared for this interview. Under a sheet of glass lay a chart of the Southern Atlantic revealing the tell-tale bulge of the West African coastline. A thin black line zigzagged from north to south like the sales curve of an unsuccessful company.

"This is the course that Captain Talbot, commander of the *Ranger*, was following," said M, following Bond's glance.

"How many people knew it?"

"The Head of Operations at Holy Loch and Captain Talbot. A copy would be 'posted' to Supreme Defence H.Q."

"So there's little chance of a leak."

"I would say none."

M struggled with the parchment and eventually anchored it with his ashtray and an imposing heavy leather pen-holder and inkwell set that Bond had never seen him use before. Bond knew better than to try to help. Once the parchment was in what M considered to be a satis-

35

factory position, he began to unfurl it laboriously. Bond watched patiently and saw a pattern beginning to emerge, identical to that on the chart but out of true, like the four-color reproduction in a cheaply produced magazine. M extended the parchment to its fullest extent and edged it to the left until the two lines mated, one on top of the other. The line on the parchment stopped at a point where there was a cross on the chart and the submarine's course had changed to the next, unfinished leg of its voyage.

"Interesting," said Bond.

"You realize what it means?"

"One of two things. Either we have a traitor, or someone can plot the course of our nuclear submarines."

M looked at his pipe and then put it in the copper ashtray. "Our communication from Cairo suggests the latter. This tracing is a sprat to catch a mackerel. Q, if he was not too busy designing rockets that could be fired from ski-sticks, could explain it better than I." It was easy to detect that M belonged to the old school. He did not entirely approve of Q's 'gadgets', as he was wont to call them. "He says there's something called 'heat signature recognition.' I can't explain exactly what it is. I've always been out of my depth with technical gobbledygook. Anyway, it works on the same principle as satellites with infrared sensors that can detect a nuclear missile in flight by its tail fire. It seems that . . . someone . . . can now locate a submerged nuclear submarine by its wake."

Bond felt the room growing colder. "And the people in Cairo. Just what are they selling? Is *Ranger* . . . what's happened to her?"

"We don't know," said M briskly. "We only know that someone in Cairo is offering to sell us a blueprint of the reputed tracking system. The whole thing may be a hoax. That's for you to find out." M did more plumbing work on his pipe. "The Chief of Staff will fill in the details. As regards the disappearance of *Ranger*, you can imagine who the first suspects are?"

Bond could. "Redland."

"And don't forget, James"—M broke off to strike a match—"sixteen Polaris missiles have a greater destructive potential than all the explosives used in the last war, including the atom bombs at Nagasaki and Hiroshima. They could blast this country into the earth so that the North Sea and the Atlantic met at Birmingham."

As if in awe of M's speech, the rain subsided to a steady drumming. Bond looked at the gray sky and thought of the England that he loved with an intensity that was almost painful.

"I'll get right on to it, sir," he said.

Chapter 5

INTRODUCING
SIGMUND STROMBERG

The room was large and splendidly furnished. The chairs in which the three men sat were deep and luxurious, and the cheerful gleam of the highly polished leather complemented the mirror sheen of the silver bowl tastefully arranged with dew-anointed red roses on the small glass-and-steel table between them. A heavy silver box lay unopened in the middle of the table and contained a mixture of Virginia and Turkish cigarettes both tipped and untipped. Thick glass carafes rested upon circular green mats. At one end of the room was a charming Romney of two small, rosy-cheeked children in Regency dress playing with a kitten.

Two of the three men were dressed in conventional suits, and there was about them an air of respectful unease. The man before them, on the other side of the table, was different; what could be seen of him was enclosed in a loose-fitting black tunic that rose to his neck like a priest's surplice without the collar. Although he was of more than average height his features were small and his mouth exceptionally so. It was like a child's mouth, with the fat Cupid's bow of the upper lip grotesquely dominating the lower. Had it been possible to turn the feature upside-down it would have looked better in the long, thin face, although its extreme narrowness would always have seemed incongruous. The short nose barely broke away from the bulbous upper lip, and one had to peer closely to see a pallid streak of near-white hairs above the watery blue eyes. The head was not prematurely bald but had never grown hair, and the small ears clung to the head like sucker fish to the side of a shark.

The two men looked at each other nervously and then studied the impassive face before them.

"Doctor Bechmann. Professor Markovitz." There was no trace of warmth in the voice. "We come to the parting of the ways ..."

Sigmund Stromberg had been conceived on Midsummer's Day in Apvorst, a small village in northern Sweden. There, the arrival of the longest day is still celebrated with dancing around the maypole and much drinking and fornication. Sigmund Stromberg was conceived as an indirect result of the second of these pursuits and a direct result of the third. His father was a fisherman, which may have had some hereditary influence on his eventual choice of career, not an immediate one, though, because his father never married his mother and as soon as the young Stromberg found himself anywhere it was with an aunt of his mother's who lived a respectful distance from Apvorst. She was a kindly woman with no children of her own, and she and her husband lavished all the love and care that they could muster on young Sigmund—the name bestowed, as was Stromberg, by his new "parents." Sigmund Stromberg was not a warm-natured child, but he worked conscientiously at school and became passionately interested in the sea. Not in ships and naval battles, like other boys, but in life below the surface. He was fascinated by fish and Frun Stromberg became disturbed by the long periods of time that the boy spent watching a fish tank in the window of a restaurant in the nearby small town of Magmo. Even on the coldest winter days young Sigmund would be staring

39

through the condensation at the speckled trout living out their last days, a look of rapt concentration on his face, his skin pinched to an onion pallor by the cold. When he was older, he obtained a piranha fish from somewhere, which he kept in a small tank in his bedroom. Frun Stromberg had no idea where the fish came from and did not ask. She was already rather in awe of her adopted son, as she chose to think of him.

At night, Sigmund would take a flashlight and go out to seek food for his pet. Frogs, toads, mice, and shrews. These were its summer fare.

One night, as she was passing his room, Frun Stromberg heard the agonized squeaks of a mouse and asked if it was necessary for the food to be fed to the fish while it was still alive. Sigmund assured her that it was. She did not believe him, but she did not argue, because when crossed, her "son" underwent a strange and disturbing metamorphosis. He would suck in his lips so that his mouth disappeared into his face to be replaced by a tiny dimple like a baby's umbilicus. His skin would turn a deathly white and his eyes suddenly fill with red as if the blood drained from his cheeks had rushed to fill their sockets. At the same time he would wrap his arms around himself and shake in silent, inchoate rage.

Frun Stromberg was frightened, the more so when she discovered Sigmund having one of his strange shaking fits before the fish tank. She wondered whether he was working too hard at school. Reports were coming in that the boy was academically brilliant, with a natural bent toward the sciences. His I.Q. was so high as to be unmeasurable.

It came as a surprise when, with all this talent at his fingertips, Sigmund started to take a keen interest in the profession of his adopted father.

Herr Stromberg was an undertaker.

Sigmund would stand in his father's workroom, much as he had stood before the fish tank, and observe the skills of the trade. The construction of the coffins, the linings, the woods that could be used, the styles and range of handles and accessories, the methods of presentation to the prospective customer.

Although she was wary of mentioning it to her husband for fear of hurting his feelings, Frun Stromberg was worried that her son's obvious talents might be wasted if he went into the family business.

She did not worry for long. Shortly after Sigmund's seventeenth birthday, the Saab in which she and her husband were travelling went out of control on a notoriously dangerous corner and plunged into a lake. Both passengers were drowned. Apparently, the brakes on the normally reliable Saab had failed.

Sigmund Stromberg was phlegmatic in the face of the tragedy that had for a second time robbed him of parents, and won the respect of the neighborhood by undertaking the funeral arrangements himself. His schoolmasters urged him to sell the business, or take on a manager, so that he could continue his studies at university and proceed to the brilliant future that seemed his by right. He disappointed them by saying that he was going to devote himself to running the business.

This he immediately began to do with great vigor, and for a young man he showed a remarkable conversance with death and what he described as its "packaging." Cremation was what he advocated as being the cleanest, purest, and most ecologically satisfactory way to go, and as business prospered he built his own private crematorium. He had to wait rather longer than anticipated for this because the firm contacted to do the business was at that time engaged in building similar, but rather larger, installations in Nazi Germany.

Stromberg became the man whose advice was always sought when there was a bereavement. Any man or woman of consequence would expect to be cremated by him and would know that in the manner of their going, the world would see ample evidence of their means. Stromberg specialized in the production of very expensive coffins with very expensive fittings. He argued—though with most of his clientele it was never necessary to argue—that the consecration of so much wealth to the flames was a kind of absolution, a purification of the body physical from the taint of Mammon before it passed into the everlasting twi-

41

light. It was the equivalent of the old Norse heroes being burned in their long boats. It also showed the world that one had money to burn.

Most clients, racked by emotion, pressed back a tear and nodded. It was only several weeks later, when the body of the loved one had been consigned to the flames and an enormous bill had arrived, that some of them thought again. But who could query, and who could quibble in such a situation? And anyway, what was there to discuss? Everything had passed into the furnace. In fact, only the corpse had been burned—usually without any gold fillings that its teeth had contained. The same coffin, which was designed like a Japanese trick box to be capable of a number of subtle variations of shape, was used again and again with a variety of gold-plated handles. Stromberg realized that few people attend so many funeral ceremonies that they would recognize one coffin from another. Some wives even assisted him by expressing a wish to be cremated in the same style of coffin as their departed husband, and this instruction he was able to fulfil to the letter.

Once the electrically controlled rollers had carried the coffin through the curtains and the hardened-steel shutter had slid to, the record of a blast furnace in operation would be turned on and the corpse quickly tipped into a plywood box reinforced with struts. The coffin would be swiftly dismantled and the corpse examined for items of value. Any fingers containing rings that had become molded into the flesh would be chopped off and the rigid mouth prised open. If it contained any teeth, and they in turn contained gold, these would be wrenched out with a pair of pliers. The "funeral assistants" would then withdraw and the true furnace sound would overlay the recorded roar preying on the minds of the mourners as they sped with restrained haste from the ghastly place of death.

It was on this grim fertilizer that the seeds of Stromberg's fortune had flourished. With the end of the war he moved his business to Hamburg where the opportunities for expansion were so much greater. But his mind was already on other things. Most of Europe's merchant fleet had been sunk during the war and Stromberg was swift to see the possibilities as Marshall Aid began to pour in to help the stricken Continent to its feet. He moved his money into shipping and was soon on smiling terms with Greeks as his first shabby cargo boats gave way to tankers. By his middle twenties, Sigmund Stromberg was a dollar millionaire.

But this was not enough. As he became richer and more successful and as his net of power and acquaintance extended, Stromberg realized that the world is not controlled by kings or presidents, but by criminals. Kings and presidents are ephemeral; organizations like Cosa Nostra and the Tongs go on for ever.

So, Sigmund Stromberg decided, he had to become a criminal. The transition was not going to be too difficult; after all, he was already a swindler, a murderer, and a corpse robber.

His opportunity arose when he learned that a number of established criminal interests had agreed on a plan to sell "insurance"—based on annual tonnage carried—to one of the richest Greek shipping magnates, with whom Stromberg had a bare acquaintance. Stromberg exaggerated the extent of his connection with the Greek and committed himself to convene a meeting at which the proposition was to be discussed by all interested parties. The meeting to take place on the *Ingemar*, at that stage the largest tanker in the Stromberg fleet.

To keep a respectful distance, Stromberg arranged that the meeting should be under the chairmanship of one Bent Krogh, who had been his right-hand man in the early crematorium days and knew all his secrets.

The decision not to attend was, as it happened, the right one because an explosion ripped apart the stateroom in which the meeting was due to take place, seconds before the arrival of the Greek. Bent Krogh and the leaders of eight of the most important criminal groups in Europe were wiped out, and the ship was turned into a blazing inferno. It was fortunate for Stromberg that the vessel was well insured.

Those who were in the know believed that the Greek had caught wind of the plan and taken his own retaliatory measures to nip any incipient protection racket in the bud. It therefore came as no great surprise when two months later, his chauffeur started the Rolls-Royce Silver Cloud and saw his legs passing his eyes as an explosion carried the vehicle, his master, and himself to a height of forty-five feet before depositing their mangled remains in a smoking crater half that depth.

Stromberg had sent a wreath to the funeral—his taste in such matters was, of necessity, exemplary—and three months later, by a series of very complicated but very logical deals, had taken over the dead Greek's shipping interests.

Now, Stromberg's cold, watery eyes flowed over the two uneasy men before him.

"Gentlemen, there is a problem."

Chapter 6

DEATH IS THE REWARD

Stromberg allowed his words to sink in and stroked a weblike fold of skin that stretched between the smallest finger of his left hand and its neighbor. He had been born with this, and Frun Stromberg had been eager to have it removed. However, even this simple operation had been beyond the family's means when Sigmund was an infant and as he grew older and more assertive he had resolutely refused to undergo surgery; he even affected the mannerism of closing the finger and thumb of the right hand around the translucent curve of flesh and tugging at it ruminatively.

"Sir, with respect, surely the technical—"

Stromberg silenced Bechmann with a gesture. "The problem is not of a technical nature. I have nothing but admiration for the work you have both carried out on the development of the submarine tracking system. The first stage of its exploitation has been conspicuously successful." He paused. "Perhaps too successful. Perhaps it has encouraged thoughts of covetousness and greed." Small beads of sweat appeared on Markovitz's forehead. Stromberg continued. "To put the matter in a nutshell, gentle-men, I have discovered that we have a traitor in the organization. Somebody who is even at this moment en-gaged in trying to sell the plans of *your* tracking system to competing international governments."

He raised an arm with a lazy, swimming motion and extended a long, bony finger behind his right shoulder. "My assistant will be able to throw more light on the matter. Fetch the evidence, Miss Chapman. From the safe in Room 4C."

The girl who appeared from the shadows had been sitting quietly taking notes since the meeting began. She was tall, dark, and slim, and by any standards, beautiful; she wore that look of haughty disdain and scarcely veiled contempt which is the hallmark of all secretaries of the rich and successful. Her black dress with the little white collar was so simple that it had come from one of the more discreet Paris fashion houses, and she moved with the casual, aristocratic grace of a pure-bred Saluki. As she left the room, Stromberg watched her approvingly.

Room 4C was long and narrow, and painted a brilliant, almost blinding white. The girl had never been in it before, and was surprised to find it empty. She had sup-posed that this was where Stromberg kept papers too secret even for her eyes. As she walked through the door she was startled by a high-pitched buzz and a red flashing light at the far end of the room. She stopped, then relaxed. It must be some kind of security device. Stromberg had sent her here, so presumably it was safe to proceed.

Drawn by the light, she strode down the room towards what looked like sliding doors. The safe must be behind them.

Suddenly there was a solid *clunk* behind her. She whirled. The door had shut. As she started towards it there was a whir of machinery and a partition fell from the ceiling like a guillotine blade, missing her by inches. The room had shrunk to a quarter of its original size.

The girl began to panic. She jabbed a finger against what she hoped desperately was an alarm button. Apart from breaking one of her long, beautifully manicured nails, she achieved nothing. There was no sound of a bell ringing.

Instead the doors slid gently aside. She was face to face with an expanse of glass that stretched from floor to ceiling. The girl shook her head, unable to believe what she was seeing. Behind the glass was water, hundreds and thousands of gallons of it. And fish, brightly colored tropical fish, darting by singly or drifting in shoals. The girl shrank back against the far wall. It was eerie down here with that enormous pressure of water behind the glass.

What was happening? Had the complex electrical system that powered Stromberg's headquarters finally broken down? Supposing the glass broke? She screamed and the noise reverberated around her prison and echoed in her ears.

"Stay calm!" She said the words out loud and peered across the tank to see if she could make out where she was. In the murk something moved. The girl saw what it was and screamed again. The nose appeared first, like a streamlined shell. Then the small pig eyes. Then the whole fish. It was a great white shark. The girl shrank back in terror and the shark sped towards her. She caught a glimpse of the two rows of jagged teeth set back beneath the pointed snout and then the fish keeled away, its white belly nearly brushing against the glass. The girl sank to her knees and started to sob hysterically. What did this nightmare mean? What in God's name was happening to her?

Crack! The sudden jolting noise was like someone freeing a window that has become frozen by frost. The glass before her lurched and water burst into the room at floor level like a sluice-gate being winched up. The water splashed against her knees and she screamed and scrambled to her feet. Her desperate hands thrust against the glass and tried to push it down but it was a pathetic, useless gesture. Her fingers slid down the glass as it re-morselessly continued to force its way upward and the rising tide of rushing water drove her skirt above her

47

lovely legs and soft, unplundered thighs. She screamed words that had no meaning and offered no hope of salvation, and as the water rose above her shoulders and her bruised head beat like a cork against the roof, the light went out and a microphone crackled into life.

"It is you who betrayed us, Kate Chapman, and you will pay the penalty!"

The water closed above the girl's head and the shark turned and sped in for the kill.

In the room above the figures of the two children in the Romney painting shivered as if in sympathy with the fate of the girl and then moved obediently to one side. Enclosed within the ornate, gilded frame of the painting was now revealed a television screen.

Bechmann and Markovitz sat with the sweat of fear sticking to their bodies and watched the screen as if hypnotized. The shark had the girl by the thigh and was worrying her like a bone. A disgusting pink candy-floss of blood spurted in all directions. For an instant, the shark's head filled the camera and it was possible to see the triangular saw teeth grinding their way through the white bone, the terrifying glint of incontestable purpose in the small, evil eye. Then the leg came away from the body and dropped slowly to the floor of the tank, leaving a corkscrew spiral of blood. The shark chased it for a moment and then turned like a whiplash to snap its mouth about the girl's waist. There was an impression of the girl's suppliant head jerking forward, the long, black hair smeared across the face, the arms pushing vainly against the brutal, gut-ripping maw. And then the stomach burst and the horrifying carnage on the screen was mercifully obliterated in a thick, red cloud.

The silence in the room was broken by a soft purr as the Romney slid back into place and two sweet and wholesome 18th-century children beamed down upon the three men in the room. Bechmann fought a desire to be sick and Markovitz wiped the sweat from his forehead with a wide bandana handkerchief.

The red slowly oozed from Stromberg's eyes and his mouth regained its normal shape. During the television transmission, the two men sitting on either side of him had been aware of an increased pattern of breathing from their employer, and on one occasion a long, sibilant hiss. Nevertheless, no sum of money on earth would have induced them to turn and look at him. The horror of the television screen was enough.

"Gentlemen." Stromberg's meticulous enunciation brought the heads swinging dutifully around. "Is there any other business?"

The words toppled one after the other like giant dominoes of ice. He rose, and neither of the men spoke.

"Good. Then you are free to leave."

When the two men had hurried from the room, Stromberg returned to his chair, made a note on his pad and pressed one of the switches on the small rectangular console in front of him. He inclined his head and spoke calmly.

"Send in Jaws."

Chapter 7

ON THE SCENT

The muted drone of the fanjets changed key and Bond felt himself projected forward as the nose of the British Airways VC10 tilted and began its long descent toward Cairo International Airport. The North African coast had been crossed west of the Ras el Kenayis, and Bond calculated that with any luck he would be on the ground within thirty minutes. Just time to review the situation and consume another dry martini. He reached above his head and pushed the call button for a stewardess. Was it a sign of growing old, or was it really true that stewardesses were not as beautiful as they used to be? The girl approached him, brushing a wisp of errant hair away from her forehead.

"Yes, sir?"

"I'd like another dry martini, please."

The girl pursed her lips and tried to remember the lesson he had taught her. "Er—that's three measures of gin—"

"Gordon's."

"—one measure of vodka—"

"Polish or, preferably, Russian."

"—shaken until it's ice-cold and then topped with a large, thin slice of lemon peel." The girl finished triumphantly.

Bond did not care for the word "topped" but he nodded agreeably. "And I'd like it in the largest glass you've got, please." Bond hated to see a good drink suffocating in a tiny glass. The martini would already be less than perfection without the addition of half a measure of Kina Lillet —a taste that his friends were always trying to cure him of, without success. There was no point in asking for it, because airlines did not carry such fundamental treasures.

Bond adjusted a stream of cool air onto his face and told himself not to be grumpy and pompous. Perhaps it was that damn medical making him feel old. He knew that he smoked far too much and was at the upper level of what a man could decently drink without being considered to have an over-reliance on alcohol. He did not need some apple-cheeked little whippersnapper fresh out of medical school leaning across a table and telling him that he was endangering his health.

Bond produced his gunmetal case and lit his fifteenth cigarette of the day.

Only the comely radiologist had introduced a note of light relief. Settling him down in his ridiculous slippers and shift, she had escorted two overweight Arabs toward their chest x-ray and said gaily, and in all innocence, "I'll be with you in a couple of shakes, Mr. Bond."

The stewardess saw Bond smile as she approached with his drink and thought how different his face suddenly looked. Something told her that he did not smile very often. It was a handsome face, but something about it frightened her. When the smile switched off, the features were cold and cruel, the eyes hard as flints. She thought that he would probably make love very well without saying anything.

Bond accepted his drink and stared down through the window at the scallop-shaped ridges of sand stretching into infinity. M was convinced that there was no chance of treachery in the U.K. Captain Talbot would have received his orders shortly before sailing, and these directly by word of mouth from Head of Operations at Holy Loch. Rear Admiral Talbot, Talbot's father, was a personal friend of M's, and his son had received the Queen's Sword at Dartmouth and done all the things expected of a young naval officer with a brilliant career in front of him. Still, although Bond respected M's judgment and would willingly have died for it, he remembered that Burgess and Maclean had also had impeccable antecedents.

The possibility of a hoax also existed. If somebody knew of the disappearance of *Ranger* they might seek to capitalize on it by pretending that they could supply the answer to the riddle in exchange for a large sum of money. This kind of thing happened whenever there was a kidnapping case with a huge ransom demand. But who would know about the disappearance of *Ranger* apart from those responsible for it? No details had been given to the press. The whole business had been given a T.S. rating.

Bond sucked the smoke from his cigarette deep into his lungs and luxuriated in its long expulsion over the empty first-class seat in front of him. Why was a *blueprint* of the tracking system being offered for sale, and not the system itself? One answer seemed more obvious than any other. Whoever was wishing to sell did not own the property he was selling. Somebody connected with an invention that could totally undermine Western defense policy had stolen the blueprint and defected.

So, who was the owner of the tracking system? Again, Bond thought he knew the answer. The Russians and their nucleus of German atomic scientists, spirited away from beneath the noses of the Allies in 1945, had been working on something like this for years. Well, now it looked as if they had cracked it. And been cracked in turn. The ghost of a smile haunted Bond's lips. Whoever had defected must have known what he was biting off. SMERSH would be humming like killer wasps. The next world war would be in the bag if the Russians could keep tabs on every Allied nuclear submarine and strike at the moment of their choice. Ninety-five percent of the free world's nuclear retaliatory strength was tied up in submarines.

Bond felt himself grow cold as he considered the picture he was painting. The Russians would walk barefoot through hell to get that tracking system back. Every airport would be under surveillance. Every spy and agent would be on twenty-four-hour alert. And what would they make of his arrival in Cairo? Especially after the Chamonix affair which Bond was more and more certain was the work of SMERSH? One thing was certain. He would have to watch his step every inch of the way.

Bond took a taxi from the airport and checked in at the Nile Hilton on the island of Roda, stuck like a lozenge in the throat of the Nile. His suite was air-conditioned and functional, and a welcome escape from the hot sun that burned down outside. He took a cold shower, changed into a blue towelling dressing gown and called room service for a long glass of tomato juice and a plate of scrambled eggs.

When this arrived, he was staring out of one of the double-glazed windows at the six-hundred-foot Cairo Tower—the tallest, and perhaps the ugliest, building in the East—and considering his first move. On the face of it, everything was very simple. A Mr. Fekkesh was the "contact," and Bond had his telephone number. Ring him up and talk business. It was like being given a list of contacts as a salesman. "Good morning, sir. My name is Bond. I represent the Great Britain Company. We're interested in old silver, antiques, and nuclear submarine tracking systems." Bond shook his head at the idiocy of it all. One day, soon, there would be a computer doing his job.

Bond finished chasing the last mouthful of scrambled egg around the plate and dressed himself in a pair of dark blue buckskin shoes purchased from Honest in the Rue Marboeuf, off-white cotton trousers, and a navy-blue silk shirt with a long collar. His cotton jacket with the propinquitous blue stripes and the single vent, made for him by someone in Hong Kong who makes such things better than anyone else in the world, he threw on the double bed.

Now, thought Bond to himself, we go to work. With a

53

sigh, he drew a table to the window and placed on it the Olivetti Lettera 32 Portable Typewriter that he now carried with him every time he travelled by air. He unzipped the cover and with the aid of a small screwdriver swiftly removed the base plate of the machine. Skillfully tucked away beneath the ribbon spools and aligned with the direction-changing arms were the dismembered skeleton grip and breach mechanism of Bond's Walther PPK 7.65 —Airline Model, as Q Branch called it. Bond unclipped the parts and put them to one side on a clean white handkerchief. Next to be removed was the cylinder. This was hollow and yielded up the barrel of the Walther, assorted pins and nuts, and forty rounds of ammunition packed in cylindrical patterns of eight. When these had been removed and placed on the handkerchief, Bond replaced the cylinder and unscrewed the nuts that held the ribbon spools in position. These were revealed as being round metal boxes camouflaged with typewriter ribbon. Each of them contained a further fifteen rounds of ammunition.

With his doctored Olivetti, Bond could bypass any airport check in the world. The machine worked when the keys were depressed and the arrangement of the Walther's constituents had been done in such a way that only the most skillful and unblasé eye would be able to detect an unfamiliar outline when the machine's working parts were exposed by an x-ray machine.

Bond deftly reassembled the Olivetti and typed "The quick brown fox jumped over the lazy dog" to make sure that it was in perfect working order. Next, he picked up the screwdriver, looked at his watch, and went to work on the gun. Precisely four minutes, forty-eight seconds later, he slapped the chamber of the assembled weapon and sat back to look at his Rolex Oyster Perpetual and expel a sigh of pleasure. It was the first time that he had beaten five minutes for the job. Bond cleaned the oil from the gun with the now soiled handkerchief and walked into the bathroom to wash his hands. He wrapped the handkerchief in two Kleenex tissues and dropped it into the waste bin.

This was the moment he loved. The moment when the adrenalin started to pump. The beginning of an assignment. To Bond it was more exciting than the beginning of a love affair. He sat down on the edge of the bed and picked up the telephone, feeling that the palms of his hands were already beginning to sweat. A girl's voice answered in Arabic and then switched to near-faultless English. Bond gave the number that he had memorized and sat back drumming his fingers on the bedside table. There was a silence and then he could hear the number ringing. And ringing.

"I'm sorry—" It was the operator's voice telling him that there was no answer. Bond was about to say he would ring again later when there was the click of a receiver being picked up. This was followed by another click, which experience told Bond meant that the call was being recorded.

" 'Alo?" It was a woman's voice.

Bond took a deep breath and started to speak. "Good afternoon. My name is James Bond. I believe you are expecting me to ring about a business matter?" There was silence at the other end of the line. "Hello?" Perhaps she did not understand English.

"You will come at six o'clock. Apartment fourteen, Semiramis Palace." The voice sounded worried. Like a child repeating a message over the telephone when its parents have gone out for the evening. "Do you know Cairo well? It is near the Citadel."

"Not terribly well, but I'll find it. Do you—?"

The continuous whine told him that the telephone had been put down.

"Were you cut off, sir?"

Bond wondered if the girl had been listening to the call. Probably. The Egyptian Intelligence Service would have an agent on the switchboard of every hotel in Cairo.

"No, it's all right, thank you."

He replaced the receiver slowly and picked up his jacket. The slight padding in the shoulder was in fact a substitute for a holster, which he now considered it unwise to carry when exposed to the attentions of hijack-happy security guards. The "padding" could be easily removed and rezipped under the armpit, or inside the waistband of

55

the trousers to form a serviceable holster for the Walther. Some speed of draw was inevitably lost. Bond had been capable of hitting a man at twenty feet in three-fifths of a second with a conventional holster draw. With the reinforced nylon, he had never broken the magic second. Still, it was better than being held up at an airport for hours while his credentials were checked out and he was eventually released with grudging apologies—or at some airports, where he might be driven away to a small room with no windows and padded walls to muffle the screams. Bond unzipped the padding, turned it inside out, and zipped it against the armpit. He put on the jacket, inserted the Walther and checked his appearance in the looking glass above the writing desk. Only a professional would notice the faint bulge. Still, he was up against professionals.

With this thought in mind, he tapped a small amount of talcum powder into the palm of his hand and applied it circumspectly to the locks of his travel-weary Vuitton suitcase and attaché case. He then wedged one of his hairs into the door of the cupboard which contained his clothes and, returning the talcum powder to the bathroom, lifted the cover of the lavatory cistern and made a small scratch at water level on the copper ball-cock, which he was pleased to see had been manufactured by Allcock and Hardisty, Bilston, Staffordshire, England. Bond knew that the tension of breaking into a man's room could reveal itself in the simplest way.

Satisfied that if anyone searched his suite he would know about it, Bond descended to the foyer and walked into the heat that even at five o'clock was striking down like a hammer. He ignored the three taxis waiting outside the hotel and turned right and then left over the El Gama, a Bridge. A hundred suffocating yards down the Shariel Corniche he found a taxi, a battered Buick that looked as if it was being driven to the scrapyard. He told the driver that he wanted to go to the Citadel and settled back uncomfortably against the imitation leather, scuffed down to its sun-bleached cross-weave. As far as he knew, he had not been followed.

The driver spoke fractured English, like a central European in an American situation comedy, and on the way Bond inquired about the imaginary addresses of a number of nonexistent friends in Cairo. Into this list he slipped the Semiramis Palace. The driver's face lit up in recognition. Yes, it was very near. That tall block of flats silhouetted against the dome of the Sultan Hassan Mosque. Bond pinpointed the building in his mind and looked ahead admiringly to the vast complex of mosques, palaces, and fortifications built just below the crest of the Mokkatam Hills. This was the Citadel of Saladin, constructed— so the guidebooks told you—over a period of seven hundred years and half a dozen conquests.

Bond paid off the driver at the outer wall and resolutely refused the blandishments of a crowd of beggars, trinket salesmen, and potential guides. It was now half-past five and, at a guess, it would take a ten-minute saunter to reach the Semiramis Palace. Just time to take advantage of the panorama from the ramparts of the Citadel. Bond climbed three flights of steps and leaned against a warm, sandstone balustrade. Below him sprawled the largest city on the continent of Africa, an untidy jumble of buildings stretching away into the heat haze like second-hand furniture at an auction, the skyline pricked by the towers of minarets and the domes of mosques.

The sky was now tinged with red, which would quickly become purple, violet, and then night. Bond watched the shadows creeping across the face of the Mohammed Ali Mosque and filled his nostrils with the alien smells that wafted up to him. To Bond, who travelled widely, smells could pinpoint a place and a mood better than sights or sounds. What was in this bittersweet odor tonight? Spices, jasmine, detritus, corruption, history? Mostly, tonight, thought Bond, it was danger—and perhaps death. He felt the reassuring pressure of the Walther PPK beneath his left shoulderblade and began to retrace his steps down the wide, worn staircase.

Chapter 8

THE SOUND OF MUSIC

The elevator was like a beautiful birdcage; an exquisite prison of thin horizontal bars interlaced with a *petit point* of ironmongery by a craftsman who was obviously a frustrated flower-arranger. It probably dated from the time of the French occupation.

The elevator carried Bond graciously and smoothly past exotic cooking smells and the plaintive wails of small children. It stopped with a decorous lurch, like an old lady steadying herself before she crossed the road, on the fourth floor. Bond slid back the two sets of metal doors and stepped out of the elevator. He listened for a moment and wondered whether anyone else had been listening to the tell-tale noise of the elevator coming up. There was no sound beyond that of a radio in one of the apartments playing some monotonous Arab dirge.

Bond moved swiftly down the stone corridor following a wavy line down the wall that looked as if it had been made by a child walking along with a pencil. He passed the door with fourteen on it and continued to the end of the corridor, where there was a door which looked as if it was not used very often. As he had surmised, this led out onto a fire escape. Worth remembering in case there was any unpleasantness. He retraced his footsteps down the corridor and stopped outside the door with fourteen on it: No sound. He knocked and waited. There was a peephole in the middle of the door, and as the seconds ticked by, he wondered whose eye would be glued to the other side. He was about to knock again when the door opened eight inches to release a whiff of unfamiliar scent.

"Bond," he said. "James Bond. You don't answer the door any faster than you do the telephone."

The girl opened the door wide and looked past him down the corridor to right and left. At a guess she was Egyptian mixed with something else—French, probably. She was beautiful, but not in a way that had ever appealed to Bond. Everything about her was slightly too big. Her mouth, her breasts, her behind—even her eyes. She reminded Bond of an overripe tropical fruit. The eyes, admittedly a devastating feature, wore too much mascara, and the bruised plum lipstick overspilled its territory by a profligate couple of millimeters. Bond looked with disapproval at the too-large gypsy earrings and the rather ridiculous sheath dress, plucked in at the waist and spreading out with false lapels to accentuate the already over-large breasts. She looked what she probably was—a high-class whore.

"I came alone," said Bond.

The girl withdrew and beckoned him into the apartment. "One must be careful." She pressed the door shut behind him and tugged at it to make sure that it was locked.

Bond looked around the apartment and decided immediately that it probably did not belong to the girl. It had an almost academic feel, with two walls covered in books and a graceful statuette. Bond admired the tall slim naked body, with the beautifully firm-small belly swelling upward like a horseshoe around the navel; the wide sweep of the eyebrows across the haughty brow, the cowl, like a judge's wig, covering the shoulders and dropping to fall just short of the erect nipples jutting out from the arrogant little breasts. This, he decided, was much more his type of woman. "I expected to be dealing with a man," he said.

"You will be." The girl turned away from the door and gestured toward another door, which opened out onto a balcony. "Mr. Fekkesh is detained at the moment. He asked me to look after you."

"Very kind of him," said Bond drily. He did not immediately move toward the balcony but picked up a framed photograph from one of the bookshelves. It showed a swarthy middle-aged man with his arms around two children who, from their appearance, must clearly be his. It was a doleful, academic face trying bravely to smile but looking overwhelmingly self-conscious. "Is this Mr. Fekkesh?" The girl nodded. "You have very attractive children."

The girl turned her head away. "We are not married." She felt it necessary to qualify the statement. "Those are not my children."

Bond tried to appear embarrassed and fumbled the photograph back onto the shelf. "I'm sorry—er, when are you expecting him back?"

"Soon. I do not know exactly. He works at the Cairo Museum. He is often late. Can I offer you a drink?"

Bond knew that she was lying and followed her out onto the balcony. Night had dropped swiftly and imperceptibly, but it was still warm. Bond breathed the spicy air into his lungs and stepped to the edge of the wrought-iron balustrade. Somewhere, someone was playing a piano. How incongruous it sounded in this Arab night. He looked down and saw light gleaming from a conservatory that jutted out from one of the ground-floor apartments. There, unmistakeably, was the silhouette of a grand piano. A figure swayed toward it.

"Noilly Prat and tonic," he said, hoping that the French influence would prevail sufficiently to make this delicious long drink available. "With a squeeze of lime, if you have it." The girl disappeared, and he made up a story about her and Fekkesh. It was something on the lines of *The Blue Angel*, and it explained why he had left his wife and

60

two children to live with an over-lush trollop. What it did not explain was how he could have anything to do with the mythical tracking system. Bond watched the million twinkling lights and the domes of the illuminated mosques and felt the acid juice of worry eating into his stomach. Out there in the big, dark, greedy city, things were happening. People were laughing, crying, making love, making deals. He, James Bond of the British Secret Service, was doing nothing. Standing on a balcony waiting to be brought a drink by someone who might have no more importance in the total scheme of things than one of those damn lights. Bond hated to feel powerless, and at the moment he was playing in a game he did not understand against people he could not see. The situation made him angry and he vowed that when the girl returned he would get some hard facts out of her. By force, if necessary.

"Your drink."

Was it his imagination or did that scent hang a little heavier in the air? Was the *décolleté* a trifle more obvious?

"Thank you."

"My name is Felicca." The voice was calmer now, and Bond noticed that the glass in her hand was half-empty. "I believe you said that yours is James?"

"I did. Twice. Once on the telephone and again at your front door." Bond's voice had a hard, cutting edge to it. "Look, Felicca. I hope you won't think me rude, but I've come a long way and I'd be very angry if I found I was on a wild-goose chase. What do you know about the tracking system?"

At the words "tracking system," the girl reacted as if touched on a nerve. Her lips parted momentarily to show the white of her teeth. "I know nothing. You must talk to Aziz—to Fekkesh. Drink your drink, make yourself comfortable." The fear was back in her voice again. "I am expecting him to ring soon."

"From the Cairo Museum?"

The girl hesitated. "Maybe."

"There are too many maybes." There was a soft pressure on his arm. The girl was holding the sleeve of his jacket

61

between finger and thumb. Her thigh moved forward purposefully and carressed the inside of his leg.

"I was asked to entertain you and I would like to do it." Her lips brushed against his cheek. "I am very good."

Yes, thought Bond, I bet you are. Good as gold. Enough gold to buy a tracking system capable of hunting down nuclear submarines. How much would that be worth? One million pounds? A hundred million?

A penumbra of light appeared around the balcony above and there was a sudden explosion of Arabic. Felicca took Bond by the hand and drew her after him through a curtain of hanging wooden beads. They were in a bedroom, although the low dais surmounted by a thin mattress and innumerable cushions owed little to Western conceptions of a bed. If the room was connected to the electric-light supply, the girl made no attempt to prove it. Her arms slid around Bond's neck like serpents and her mouth trembled like that of a volcano about to erupt. If a kiss is pressure applied by one volatile surface upon another, then Bond was kissed everywhere and with everything. The hot, soft lips circulated, the breasts rotated, and the belly churned. Felicca was right—she was good at it.

Bond drank of the nectar and then dashed the vessel from his lips. With a quick jerk of his arms he broke her grip and threw her down on the cushions. Felicca stared up at him, her right hand slowly moving to her bruised left shoulder. Her eyes asked the question shortly before her mouth did. "Why?"

"I didn't come here to make love to you. Stop beating about the bush and tell me where Fekkesh is." Felicca's skirt had risen to the level of her thighs and Bond could see why Fekkesh had decided that life had more to offer than the four thousand years of history encompassed by the Cairo Museum. He yanked her roughly to her feet and shook her until her dress dropped off her shoulders. "Don't think I wouldn't hurt you, don't—!"

In retrospect it seemed strange. Bond could remember looking at the gun for seconds. He had seen the slight movement of the wooden beads as it was thrust between them. Heard the death rattle of their clicking. Established

62

the make of the gun—a Japanese M14. Seen the finger tightening around the trigger and the whole hand contracting to ensure that the shot was not jerked away at the last instant.

In reality the whole image could only have been before his eyes for a fraction of a second. Then the girl was propelled into his arms as if by the point of a javelin. The hideous thump that ran through his own body as if his arms were shock-absorbers. Then the dead-weight collapse. The rattle at the back of the throat. The warm blood pumping through his fingers. Bond threw himself sideways, still using the girl as an unintended shield. Two more shots thudded into the wall beside his head, and he rolled over twice and tore out the Walther. Thank God it was dark in the room. He fired blind onto the terrace, and a string of beads whipped away like a serpent. Silence, save for the chinking of the wooden beads. Was the gunman waiting for him on the terrace? Bond edged his way around the wall and waited with his back beside the opening. The light had gone out on the balcony above. He could imagine the neighbors wondering what had happened, debating whether to call the police. Deciding to do nothing. Far below there was still the tinkle of that damn piano. What tune was it playing? The notes rose up like soap bubbles. "Moonlight Becomes You." Bond permitted himself a grim smile. No point in staying here. The gunman had probably escaped immediately after the shooting. Let himself out of the apartment by the front door. Bond judged the distance and his line of departure and then threw himself through the bead curtain. Three strides, and he was in the first room he had entered. Nobody. The outer door shut. Was there any point in going down the fire escape or should he go back to the girl? Better the girl. If she died and Fekkesh did not turn up, then he was finished. And he did not want to get involved with the Egyptian police. There would be a lot of questions, and he would be asking none of them.

It was then that he heard the sigh. At first he thought it was the girl, but unless she had crawled out onto the balcony, it was too close. Bond switched off the light and moved along the wall to the balcony. Still in shadow, he peered out. At first there seemed to be nothing—and then, a hand. Knuckles straining white as they clung desperately to the bottom of one of the railings of the balustrade. Another bloodstained hand dragged itself like a half-crushed spider toward the M14, lying like a tempting prize beneath the guard rail. Bond's blind shot must have wounded the man. He had tried to scramble back along the balconies to the corner of the building and slipped. Now, like a good professional, he was trying to save his life and take Bond's. An elbow found a precarious perch on the parapet, and the hand clawed forward toward the butt of the gun. Bond could see the clenched teeth, the intense wrinkling of the brow. There was a smell of cordite and sweat in the air—the sweat that a man gives off when he is close to death. The man's fingers brushed against the gun and then, in a desperate flurry of movement, sought to scratch it backwards to where it could be seized. As a background to the spectacle, the distant pianist had offered up a medley of Rodgers and Hart numbers.

Bond could not help feeling admiration for the single-minded purpose of the man who had been sent to kill. He was trying to do his job. Bond stepped out on the balcony as the man's hand finally closed about the gun. Their eyes met for the fraction of a second that can be an infinity, and Bond fired twice. The man disappeared as if tugged from below. There was a pause and then the sound of shattering glass and a reverberating thump extending into a long, jangling discord. Then a woman screaming. Bond went to the parapet and looked down. There was an untidy hole in the conservatory roof, and the body of the assassin could be seen spread-eagled across the grand piano. The screams increased in intensity, and lights began to go on. Inspired by the arrival of her unexpected accompanist, the woman was having hysterics.

Bond ducked back into the bedroom and switched on the light. This time, the police would be called. He had to move fast. Felicca was lying with her face in a pillow, and for a moment he thought that she was dead. Her face was gray and her whole body seemed to have shrunk. It was as if the bullet had punctured her spectacular buoyancy. Now she looked like another person. Vulnerable, defeated.

Maybe I was wrong about you, thought Bond. Maybe you do love Fekkesh. Maybe that is why you got involved, and found yourself getting out of your depth. One thing is for certain: the water is closing over your head.

Bond held the girl's shoulder and pressed his mouth to her ear. His voice was low and urgent. "Felicca. Where is Fekkesh?" No answer, but the mouth trembled. "I may be able to help him to stay alive. That man won't be alone. There'll be others. They're probably after him now."

A tear formed in the girl's eye and rolled slowly down her cheek. Who was she crying for? Herself? Fekkesh? The world of greed and hatred, and folk like James Bond? Bond squeezed her shoulder and despised himself. The girl was dying, dammit! He should be ringing for a doctor, not prising her secrets out of her.

"Tell me. I can save him."

The girl's mouth opened and closed like that of a dying fish. "He is meeting someone. At the pyramids. *Son-et—*"

Her head fell sideways, and Bond felt the life rush from the body. He laid her back against the cushions and rose swiftly to wash the blood from his hands.

Chapter 9

DEATH OF A SALESMAN

"You have come tonight to the most fabulous and celebrated place in the world . . ."

The male voice was cold and almost condescending. With the assistance of fourteen loudspeakers it began to swell dramatically. "Here, on the plateau of Gizeh, stands forever the mightiest of human achievements. No traveller —emperor, merchant, or poet—has trodden on these sands and not gasped in awe."

Like a gas-jet being turned up, light slowly flooded the eastern face of the Pyramid of Cheops. There was an obedient and reverential murmur from the serried rows of tourists as their heads tilted back and their eyes rose four hundred and fifty-five feet into the night sky.

All the tourists except one.

Major Anya Amasova, sitting at the end of the fifth row with an empty seat beside her, took advantage of the sudden burst of light to check that the two men assigned to her by General Nikitin were in position. They were. Standing, it seemed to her, self-consciously, at either diagonal

66

of the audience. They were both looking up at the enormous, overpowering structure, taking advantage of the unexpected history lesson. Instantly, they were snatched from view as the lighting changed, throwing the pyramid into silhouette.

"The curtain of night is about to rise and disclose the stage on which the drama of a civilization took place . . ."

Anya looked at her watch. Fekkesh was late.

To the left, the Sphinx slowly appeared as if illuminated by the first rays of dawn. There was an admiring gasp from the audience in which Anya found herself joining. It was impossible not to be moved in these surroundings. Disconcertingly so. She should not have agreed to this meeting place.

"With each new dawn I see the Sun-god rise on the banks of the Nile. His first ray is for my face, which is turned toward him."

Bond stood in the shadows, listening to the neutered voice of the Sphinx and wondering if the Pharaoh Chephren had really talked like that. Still, perhaps the sculptors and the *metteurs en scène* of the *son-et-lumière* knew better. There was certainly something sexually ambiguous about the Sphinx.

When light permitted, Bond sorted through the rows of tourists looking for Fekkesh. Only the beautiful, erect girl in the fifth row did not seem to belong to a tour party. Poor devils, he thought, Cairo, Gizeh, Memphis, El Amarna, Abydos, Luxor, Karnak, Aswan. Five thousand years of history in three weeks, two donkey rides, and a bout of gastroenteritis.

". . . and for five thousand years I have seen all the suns men can remember come up into the sky . . ." The girl in the fifth row was worth concentrating on. It was impossible to see her clearly, but there was a quality of luminosity about her that drew her forward from the lumpy women with clumsy cardigans draped around their sunburned shoulders. But maybe this was not the best time to be a girl-watcher. Similarly placed to himself were two men wearing lightweight suits that looked as if they had been made out of cardboard boxes. They appeared uncomfortably out of place—like Toby mugs amongst Dresden shepherdesses. They looked like the kind of failed Bulgarian weightlifters that Redland recruited to eliminate enemies of the State. Maybe they were friends of the man on the concert grand who would never find anyone to play a duet with him.

Bond was concentrating on the two men when he saw something that made him draw back into the shadows. As a patch of light hit the Pyramid of Chephren, a small man with hunched shoulders appeared on the other side of the audience from Bond. His head started nodding as he counted the rows of seats. Bond could not be certain, but he thought he recognized the face he had seen in the photograph at the flat.

Then the lights went out.

Anya recognized Fekkesh immediately and breathed a sigh of relief. He was standing within ten feet of her, looking nervous and insecure as he always did. She wondered if he remembered where she had said she would be. Yes. His eyes were travelling to the right-hand corner of the audience and methodically counting back. One, two, three, four, five. His smile was more one of relief than welcome. He stepped forward, and she moved her knees to let him pass. Then he stopped. His face registered transparent fear as if he had suddenly seen a ghost, and he turned on his heel. Anya half rose to her feet as he hurried away into the shadows.

Then the lights went out.

Bond cursed and started to run toward the back of the audience. In the darkness, his feet caught against a cable, and he tripped and nearly fell. He cursed again, and there was an impatient "Ssh!!" from the hypnotized onlookers. Why the hell had Fekkesh taken off like that? Whom had he seen? Could he have recognized Bond? Hardly likely. One of the heavies? Possibly. Bond abandoned speculation and concentrated on running as fast as he dared. A sudden blaze of an illumination on the Pyramid of Mycerinus showed him a figure and its grotesquely larger shadow running down the north side of Cheops. By some strange, optical illusion, the shadow seemed to be moving

68

out of time with its owner, almost as if giving chase to it. Bond pulled out his Walther and sprinted, the distorted voices from the amplifiers tearing at his ears as he ran past. Now it was dark again. God! This was like the night barrage before the Battle of El Alamein. The blinding flashes of the twenty-five pounders throwing into relief the advancing infantry.

As if to demonstrate the image, the Sphinx was once more illuminated, and as Bond's eyes were automatically drawn toward the source of light he saw a sight which brought him abruptly to a halt. Silhouetted against the distant Sphinx was a giant figure which at first glance seemed like some statue, unrecorded since the dawn of history. Its head was huge and ungainly, and its arms stood away from the body in the pose of a wrestler flexing to take hold of an opponent. Viewed behind it, the Sphinx seemed an appropriate mount to bear this Colossus away across the desert. And then the giant moved. The head swivelled toward Bond, the eyes blazed, and the light shone from its mouth as from a lighthouse.

And then everything was plunged into darkness.

Fekkesh was desperate. Desperate as a man who has taken out a mortgage he cannot repay, or gambled in a card game when the stakes are too high, or promised a woman he loves something he can never give her. But most of all, he was desperate because he knew that his time was running out, that he was going to die. When he found the opening in the wall, he pressed into it like a bug into a crack. Anywhere, to get away from the big man who killed for Stromberg. Why? *Why* had he listened to them? What had they been able to do to him to make him believe that he could ever turn against Stromberg and get away with it? Especially with this. It was too big. He had been insane. He should have stayed on the fringe. Taken the money, been grateful.

Something impeded the passage of air to his nostrils, and Fekkesh froze. The man was standing in the opening. In the darkness, the sound of his heavy breathing sounded like the sawing of wood. At that moment, Fekkesh gave up the ghost. He hunched his shoulders and began to whimper. God, please make it quick, he prayed. Please spare me too much pain. He thought of his children and of Felicca, waiting at the flat, but most of all, his mind was full of a blind inchoate terror that numbed him like an injection sinking deeper and deeper into his gums. He pressed his eyes tight shut and dug his nails into his palms. God, let it happen soon. He was tightening like a spring that had to break.

When the hand fell upon his knee, it was almost a relief. He braced himself and opened his eyes. The outline of the face was visible against the stars. There seemed to be no malice in it. No hatred. No cruelty. If this was the face that animals wore before they ate each other, then it was not too bad. And then the mouth opened and Fekkesh saw the two rows of jagged, stainless-steel teeth. And then he started screaming. And Jaws pulled him down like a rag doll upon the scaffold of his knee and bit through the back of his neck as easily as if it had been a stick of celery.

To Bond, the noise that ended the screams was like that of a stick breaking. He raced toward it and arrived as the huge man materialized from between two blocks of stone like a spirit escaping from some unrifled sarcophagus. For a second the two men faced each other, and then Jaws showed his gleaming teeth in a contemptuous smile and turned on his heel to be swallowed up by the night. Bond hesitated, torn between the knowledge that he must find Fekkesh and an impulse to pursue this terrifying giant with the gleaming teeth. There was no choice. Fekkesh came first. Bond held his gun low and edged his shoulder around one of the thirty-ton blocks of stone that formed the base of the pyramid. His heart sank as he saw a foot protruding from the shadows. He knelt down swiftly and felt for the man's heart. Something glistened in the darkness; a pool of blood was spreading from the neck and shoulders. Someone, there were no prizes for guessing who, must have chopped half through the man's neck. Bond forgot about the heart and pushed back the man's head. The face with the wide staring eyes was recognizable. Fekkesh.

Swiftly and skillfully Bond went through the pockets

70

of Fekkesh's shabby suit. The breast pocket yielded a small diary. Bond quickly felt inside his own jacket and produced a silver pencil with a number of modifications by Aspreys. Two presses of the clip turned it into a flashlight. Bond flicked through the diary with the aid of its thin beam. The address section was empty, and there were no telephone numbers. The day-to-day entries seemed all connected with work. Bond's sketchy Arabic unscrambled "Meeting of Khem-en-du Excavation Committee" and a luncheon appointment with the directors of the Coptic Museum. There was even a note to remember Felicca's birthday. Some tiny and nearly dried-up reservoir of sentiment in Bond was pleased to see that this date had passed. He hoped the lovers had enjoyed it.

There was an entry for the following Thursday: "Max Kalba, Mujaba Club. 7.30 pm." Neither the name nor the club meant anything to Bond, but it was the only lead he had unless he searched Fekkesh's flat and could get into his office at the Cairo Museum. That, and find the big man. There could not be many countries in the world where he would find it easy to hide in a crowd. Bond shivered as he looked down at the broken body at his feet. How could the neck have been torn open like that? It was almost as if—no. He rejected the suggestion as being too horrible, too absurd. But, there again, he had once examined a rat after a terrier had killed it and—almost against his will, Bond's gaze dropped once more to the bulging eyes, the thin sharp-nosed features, the blood beginning to coagulate around the jagged puncture marks. Fighting a desire to be sick, he thrust the diary into his pocket and turned away from this place of terrible death.

Outside, it was dark and the only sound was the distant one of car doors slamming and tour operators calling the faithful to get into their Russian-built coaches. The *son-et-lumière* must be over. Bond brushed the sand from his knees and began to walk around the great black bulk of Cheops to where the car headlights were sawing at the darkness. What had Napoleon calculated? That there was enough stone in the three pyramids of Gizeh to build a wall ten feet high around France—Bond preferred to deal

71

in feet even when the calculations were being made by Napoleon.

Bond heard the soft footfall in the sand too late, and turned the wrong way. A flash of lightning struck him behind the right ear and a deep pit opened up at his feet. He tumbled slowly into it and looking back as he rolled over and over could see that the triangular face of Cheops was rising, not four hundred and fifty-five feet into the sky, but forever until it blotted out the heavens like a great black cliff.

Chapter 10

SHOCK TACTICS

Somebody was tapping on Bond's head and asking to come in.

The sound was a long way away and heard through many closed doors, but it was distinctive and persistent. Bond waited, hoping that whoever it was would go away, but the sound continued, rhythmic and jarring. With each tap a tiny filament of pain ran through Bond's brain. It was no good. He would have to see who was there. Grumbling to himself, he began to force his eyes open. How difficult it was. He must have been deep in sleep. Curse them for disturbing him. Now, who was there in the thick, swirling mist? Bond screwed up his eyes to concentrate. The face was like a halloween mask, round and shiny, with two deep-socketed eyes that seemed to be pouring out rivulets of tears. The tears fell like twin cascades to be sucked into the recessed corners of a broad, straight mouth thatched with a white mustache of horizontal hairs. Bond was puzzled. None of the features moved. And there was no nose. And the strange luster of the perfect round face. It was shiny. Shiny as a button.

Slowly, Bond's mind cleared and he realized what he was looking at. One of the buttons on the shirt of the man who was standing in front of him.

"He is conscious." The voice was Russian.

A rough hand jerked Bond's head backwards and he looked into a square, clumsily featured face that might have been whittled with a blunt penknife. So, the two men at the *son-et-lumière* had been Russians. At least, this one was. Bond did not say anything, but concentrated on clearing his head and testing the rope that secured his hands behind the back of a chair. It must have been tightened nearly to the bone. His ankles were also bound to the two front legs of the chair. This was ominous. The more so when one examined the apparatus that the second man was connecting to a heavy-duty battery. It was a small metal box with an on/off switch and a glass panel showing a red-calibrated dial. There was also a lever, currently resting at the top of its vertical slot and, most sinister of all, two long thin wires leading away from the side of the box and ending in metal claws.

Bond forgot about the throbbing lump on the back of his head. He knew what the box was, and he knew what they were going to do to him. The man who had been connecting the battery leads stood up and nodded to his companion. They were ready. There was no sign of the big man.

Bond looked around the shabby, featureless room and tried to find items to concentrate on. If you were being tortured it helped to focus on something. Direct yourself away from the agony and the information you were supposed to be giving to some totally unrelated, meaningless object. Bond's eyes glanced off the naked lightbulb and lit upon a calendar on the far wall. It showed the Egyptian version of a pin-up, a pretty black-haired girl showing her face but nothing else and extending a shy hand toward a motor scooter. She gazed at Bond as she must have gazed at the cameraman, not quite certain what either of them was doing. Yes, she would do. They would see this thing through together.

"Mr. Bond." It was a surprise to hear his own name,

and spoken in good English with only the faintest trace of accent. "The answer to one simple question can save you excruciating pain and mutilation. Where is the blueprint of the tracking system?" Despite his predicament, Bond felt like laughing out loud. "I don't have the tracking system."

The man holding the metal claws began to tap them together like castanets.

"Then why did you kill Fekkesh?"

The question threw Bond. They had killed Fekkesh. The big gorilla with the mouth like a barracuda had chewed a hole out of his neck. What were they getting at? They must be laying some kind of trap. Did they think that Fekkesh had handed over the blueprint before he was killed? Or perhaps hidden it somewhere for Bond to find? That must be it. They wanted to tie up the loose ends.

Bond took a deep breath before replying because he knew that his answer was going to cause him a lot of pain.

"Sorry, chum. You've drawn the same answer. I didn't kill him." No flicker of emotion passed through the man's face. He shrugged and then bent forward and started to unbuckle Bond's belt. Bond's stomach froze. If the beads of sweat that were pouring off him ran over it they would turn into icicles. He looked toward the man standing by the metal box and then turned away. The man's eyes were glistening lasciviously. Pain was his mistress. The top of Bond's trousers was unhooked and the buttons undone one by one. He was like a child being taken to the lavatory. Then the trousers and underpants were pulled down to his knees. Bond sought the surprised eyes of the girl in the calendar. It was strange but he felt embarrassed looking at her. She was like the girl at the dentist's who hands you a glass of pink water that your numb mouth finds it difficult to spit into. Her disdaining smile apologizes for your clumsiness.

"This is your final chance. Where is the microfilm?"

"Go—yourself!!"

The man did not reward Bond's obscenity with a slap across the face. He was a professional, and he could afford to conserve his energy. An electric current passed through

75

the genitals is a million times more effective than beating a man's face to a bloody pulp. He stood back and his accomplice hurried forward with the claws. There was about him an indecent, scuttling haste, like a crab closing with a cracked mollusk. His breath stank and Bond turned his head away from the noisome odor. He glimpsed the claws sprung wide and then winced as the metal closed about his soft flesh. This pain was bad enough. How could he stand more?

The operator bit his lip for an instant and then returned to the machine. He moved his hand to the on/off switch and then turned to Bond as if to photograph him in repose. Bond could feel him estimating how much give there was in the ropes. How far Bond's tortured, screaming body would be able to leap into the air. Then, he pressed down the switch.

Immediately, Bond felt a nerve-jangling tremor fanning out from the most sensitive of his organs. It was not a pain, but it set his teeth on edge. The machine had come to life and was saying that it was ready to inflict agony. Bond concentrated on the girl in the calendar and tried to bury himself deep in her soft, brown eyes.

"You are stupid, Mr. Bond. Because, in the end, you are going to tell us everything we want to know." Bond's gaze did not deviate. "We will start slowly, just to give you a taste of what is to come."

Keep looking into the kind brown eyes. The nice lady is trying to sell you a motorcycle. With a motorcycle you could drive away from this room and never come back. You could—

The scream left Bond's body as if it was taking most of his vital organs with it. He felt his body dismantling to make way for its passage through his throat, but his throat wasn't big enough. The scream escaped through his brain, through his ears. Everywhere. He had been prepared for pain, but this was too horrible. It was a physical invasion of his body. It was unlike anything he had ever experienced before. As if his whole nervous system had been turned over with a sharpened spade.

"You see." The voice came through the mists of purple

pain. "It is not pleasant, is it? And it can go on, and on, and on." Bond's body was awash with sweat. He could feel it dripping down onto his chest. There was a cruel throbbing from his wrists telling of the strain he must have put on his tightly tethered hands when the current threw him forward. "But do not despair. It is when you can no longer feel that you should become worried. For then you will no longer be a man." God save me, thought Bond. Is there any force on earth or in heaven that can pluck me from this crucifying rack of pain? "Would you rather talk now, or later?"

Bond pulled his head up and once more focused on the calendar. Come on, sweetheart. We can do better than this. I thought we had something beautiful going between us. I thought we were on the brink of something—

This time, Bond was prepared for the wave of pain. It swept in like a rising tide, probing familiar ground, infiltrating pre-explored crevasses. And then it edged forward, overlapping itself to invade new territory. Saturating unexplored sand, drawing forth new screams of seared, screeching agony. The hinges of Bond's mouth snapped back and his throat divided into the columns of an organ as he hurled himself forward against the cruel ropes. The roman candle of pain between his legs was burning out his soul.

"*Nyet!*"

The waves fell back and the sea of suffering slowly withdrew as if sucked down some vast distant plug hole. Bond, head on sweat-soaked chest, strained his throbbing ears for another sound of that female voice.

"Fools! Imbeciles! Are you trying to kill him?" She was speaking Russian, but Bond could keep pace with her. His time for a diploma at the defector Vozdvishensky's language symposium for employees of the Ministry of Defense had broken all records. "What information can he yield us dead?" There was an immediate murmur of disgruntled disapproval. Bond opened one eye, straining to catch sight of this newcomer. He saw two slim trouser legs, one petulant heel tapping against the floor. "Must I remind you again who is in control of this operation?

Untie him and revive him. We have drugs that can do this work." Not entirely an altruist, thought Bond.

"But, Major. With respect." The voice belonged to the senior torturer and had precious little respect in it. "We have experience of these methods. We have enjoyed much success with them. The man will not die until we want him to."

"Nevertheless. Do as I say!"

Bond gambled that all eyes would be upon the speaker, and turned his head slightly. Through half-closed eyes he could make out an erect female presence that was familiar. The girl he had seen at the *son-et-lumière*. So, she was one of them. Not one of them, but in control of them. He could understand the reaction of the others. Having to receive orders from a woman after years of torturing people their way. Why couldn't she find a job in a factory or on a collective farm? God knows, they needed all the help they could get.

Bond continued to push back the heavy curtains of throbbing, aching pain and stifled the scream that rose to his lips as the claws were plucked from his flayed organ. He heard a knife click open, and the blade began to saw through the ropes about his ankles. This was it. His only chance was approaching. If he didn't make a move soon, he was finished. They would open him up by one means or the other, and when they found there was nothing inside, they would kill him. The girl wasn't being squeamish, she was being practical.

Bond risked another glance. The operator of the machine was sulkily wrapping the connection wires around his fingers. Suddenly the mist of pain rose as it was penetrated by the bright sunlight of an idea. It might work. It just might work. Bond lolled forward and felt the knife sawing through the ropes at his tortured wrists. Halfway through, three-quarters, seven-eighths. He braced himself and, as the rope parted, hurled himself forward toward the hideous instrument of torture that had set out to emasculate him. It was still humming, and a red light glowed. Too late, the operator saw what was in his mind and desperately sought to free his fingers from the enveloping wire. Bond drove the lever down so that it buckled against the bottom of the slot. The needle on the gauge leaped forward and with a bright flash the man's body jackknifed in the air. There was a two-tier scream and a disgusting smell of burning, frizzled flesh. The man's features flattened against the wall with a sickening, blood-smearing crunch, but he was dead one twentieth of a second before the impact.

Instinctively, Bond ducked to one side and the knife arm flashed past his throat. With automatic deference to the classic defense riposte, his right arm cut across and his body swivelled with it. The two forearms met halfway between the two bodies and the withdrawing knife arm was jarred to one side. Bond saw the opening and drove hard and upward. His stiff, locked wrist travelled two feet and the heel of his left hand, with the fingers spread wide for extra rigidity, came up under the spokesman's throat with terrifying force. He staggered back, and in the same instant, Bond lashed out with the edge of his finger-locked hand turned into an axe blade. The blow hacked into the Adam's apple in the middle of the taut throat, and the man fell like a tree.

Bond looked down at the two untidy heaps of human being and wondered how long it would be before streams of homeless vermin started to leave their bodies. The girl was staring at him as if mesmerized by the events of the last few seconds. Bond fastened his trousers and looked at her just long enough to see that she was beautiful and not pointing a gun at him.

"Thanks for saving my life." He smiled grimly, and added as an afterthought—"And possibly one or two other people's."

And then he was through the door and down the worn stairs, two at a time, throwing his weight against a second door and feeling the blessed cool of the night air. He ran hard down an alley and then out into a street where people were walking and he could slow down and walk amongst them, listening to his pumping heart reassuring him that he was still alive.

Chapter 11

ADVENTURES IN CLUBLAND

The Mujaba Club was an incongruous building to find in a bustling tourist metropolis on the eastern bank of the Nile three hundred and seventy-five miles south of Cairo—for that was where Bond eventually found it—on the outskirts of Luxor. It was surrounded by clumps of palm trees, to be sure, but that, apart from its awnings and shutters, was its only obvious concession to the mystic East. In all other respects it was redolent of the era when Britannia ruled the waves and most of the land that divided them. It looked like a cross between an open prison, a Methodist church hall, a youth hostel, and the officers' mess of an inferior county regiment, and, because it was none of these things, yet clearly built by English hands, it had to be a club.

Bond was feeling less depressed. He was not a masochist, but the pain and relentless action of two nights before had left him with a keen edge of purpose. He had a lead, something to go on, something to get his teeth into. Most important of all, there was a tough, ruthless game being played for enormous stakes, and he had been dealt in. No matter the insignificance of his cards. What was vital was that he should have the chance to play them.

Outside the club was an impressive range of cars. Bond noted the large Mercedes and the latest Cadillac which must have been flown over from the States almost before it was available to the American public. There was clearly a lot of money about. Most of it, from the look of the number plates, Arabic. Bond squared his shoulders beneath the sculptured lightness of his black barathea dinner jacket and met the eye of the garishly dressed doorman. The man wore a curved dagger in a scabbard of semiprecious stones tucked into the waistband of his embroidered burnous. He had a nose like a falcon, and his sharp, dark eyes ran over Bond like the editor of *Burke's Peerage* considering an applicant for a vacant baronetcy. Bond passed muster and returned the slight inclination of the head that passed him through to the interior of the club.

Inside, the atmosphere was considerably more gracious than Bond had anticipated from his first observation of the building. The entrance hall was high and vaulted, with cloakrooms and a telephone room going off to the right. On the left was a reception desk, now untenanted, a notice board, and another board covered in green beige and criss-crossed with brass-studded pink tape which held letters to members. Bond inspected the notice board. There were details of camel races and of a book being made on competitors in the club's backgammon tournament. Bond quickly scanned the list of names, but there was no sign of a Kalba, Max or otherwise. Better to ask, and best to ask with a drink in one's hand.

The bar was another pleasant surprise. Spacious, comfortable, and with the minimum concession to Arab kitsch. A long mirror-backed bar ran along one wall, and there were groups of tables and low-backed armchairs and cushioned window seats. Two fans in the ceiling turned slowly and silently. Through a door at the far end could be seen a candle-lit dining room with waiters in short tunics and deep purple waistcoats. One or two couples were already studying menus. Bond settled himself at the bar and ordered a vodka martini. The dress of the people about him was interesting. Some of the men wore dinner jackets; others affected traditional costume, and their strong aquiline features could barely be seen emerging from their white robes and flowing headdresses. For the most part, they sipped daintily from tiny cups of coffee and talked eloquently with their hands whilst their womenfolk sat silent and respectful, only their dark, almond eyes taking off to make whirlwind sorties around the room. They were beautiful, these women, thought Bond, perhaps more so than the Europeanized ones with pendant jewelry hanging from their foreheads. So much of their mystery was still hidden, and only those darting eyes spoke of immortal longings awaiting satisfaction.

But, enough of this ethnic speculation. There was work to be done. Bond finished his drink and raised a finger to catch the barman's eye. And then he saw her. Reflected in the long mirror behind the bar. The girl at the *son-et-lumière*. The girl whose intervention two days before had saved his life. She was coming into the room like a clipper under full sail, and she looked magnificent. Her dress was a long, black, wispy thing that trailed behind her and stopped just below the graceful line of her slim shoulders. Her fine breasts jutted out proudly. Her hair was jet black and lustrous, and there was no touch of artifice about the way it hung casually to form a natural, jagged frame to her face. The face was beautiful, and Bond looked at it properly for the first time. The eyes were a deep blue, almost violet, beneath dark brows. The slender nose had a suspicion of a tilt, and the mouth was both positive and sensual. In fact, the whole face had an air of determination and independence helped by the set of the high cheekbones and the fine line of the jaw. This sense of purpose was carried through to the way she moved. She held herself proudly yet unselfconsciously, and moved through the room as if it was a vassal state to be crossed on the way to defeat an enemy. She held her flat, black evening bag like a weapon.

With a pang of sadness, Bond realized that this girl reminded him of someone he had once loved and married.

Tracy had been fair, and this girl was dark, but there was about their faces those same qualities of courage, spirit, and resourcefulness that Bond prized above all others in a woman. But a voice of caution shouted in Bond's ear. Steady on! This girl is a Russian. She is almost certainly a member of SMERSH and is therefore a deadly enemy. Her presence here is not programmed by Eros but whatever poor, demented god controls the movements of spies and double agents. Beware!

Taking the advice of his conscience, Bond dismissed the hovering barman and slid from his stool. Three steps and he was by the girl's side.

"Good evening. What an unexpected pleasure."

"Commander Bond." She had the grace to smile, and even if it was false, the effect was still stunning.

"You have the advantage of me once again. Please allow me to buy you a drink."

Anya looked into the handsome, cruel face with a sense of *déjà vu*. Was it only in the last two days and in the file marked *Angliski Spion* at the Department of Military Records that she had seen this man before? As she allowed herself to be steered toward the bar she could understand why he was the most respected as well as feared of the British agents. His body seemed to flow rather than move in a series of programmed steps. He was like a panther or some other animal that lived by speed and stealth— and death.

"I think our meeting deserves celebration, don't you?" Bond did not wait for a reply but ordered the best champagne. It came in the form of a bottle of Taittinger '45. Anya felt his cold eyes appraising her body. "You look very beautiful," he said. "Perhaps electrifying would be a better word."

Anya stretched out her hand for her glass. "I am sorry. That is not the way I would have handled it."

Bond permitted himself a dry smile and raised his glass. "Thank you." His mind was racing What was the girl doing here? Had he been followed? If they had still wanted him, why hadn't they picked him up in Cairo? It would have been easier. Perhaps there was some strange grain of comfort in her presence. Fekkesh's diary had been taken from his pocket at the Cheops Pyramid. If the girl was following up the Kalba lead it could mean that there was something in it. It could also mean that Kalba's life expectancy was only slightly longer than that of Fekkesh. He had better find the man quickly. And was the girl alone?

Bond lowered his glass and looked into the dangerously deep blue eyes. "You must be lonely without your boy-friends."

"They are easily replaced."

Bond tried again. "What a coincidence that we should both decide to visit the Mujaba Club tonight."

"Life is full of coincidences, Commander Bond."

Bond shouldered the angels aside. "Who are you? How do you know me?"

The girl threw back her head and again Bond was captivated, almost against his will, by the fine determined line of her jaw. "My name is Major Anya Amasova, and I am employed by the Defense Department of the Peoples' Republic. We have lists of murderers in many countries."

"Most of them working for you, I would imagine," said Bond. "Please, let's spare ourselves any more of that kind of facile recrimination. I imagine we're both in the same line of business, and it could become very tedious."

Anya's lips set in a tight line that almost robbed them of their sensual bulge. Her eyes blazed. "You will not talk to me like that!"

Bond glanced quickly at his watch. It was ten past seven. "Not this evening, I won't." He stood up and slid some money across the bar. "You must excuse me, I have work to do. It made a delightful change to meet you informally."

"The pleasure was entirely yours." Anya did not return the curt nod but expelled the pent-up breath of anger as Bond moved away from her. What a brute of a man. Overweening, sardonic, facetious. And yet . . . ? She asked herself whether she was not perhaps overreacting. Was there not some small, despised part of her that found him attractive, for all that? Was there not about him that same, unfathomed, dangerous quality that had so immediately drawn her to Sergei? She blushed at her perfidy to State and lover. She must pull herself together. The mission had so far been considerably less than a success and if the Presidium knew of the full extent of her incompetence they would not hesitate to deal with her severely. The killing of Boris and Ivanov was going to be difficult enough to explain without her failure to close negotiations for the microfilm. Tonight might be her last chance.

Bond entered the dining room trying to clear his mind and think coolly and logically. Damn the woman! Why did she have to be so consummately beautiful? Where did the Russians find such creatures? Did they have some secret factory in the Urals where they manufactured them? And her English was so good. Hardly a trace of accent. And that dress. That didn't come from one of the "closed shops" specially reserved for key State personnel.

"Yes, sir?" the maître d'hôtel was standing at his side.

"I don't want a table. I'm trying to find one of your members. A Mr. Max Kalba."

The man's eyebrows lifted. "Mr. Kalba is the *owner* of the Mujaba Club, sir. I think you'll find him in the private gaming room."

Bond felt the adrenalin pump. Now, perhaps, he was getting somewhere. He left the dining room by a side entrance, following the directions given him by the maître d'hôtel, and walked along a deep-carpeted corridor. The building must be built in the shape of an L. On the right, through an open door, he could see the familiar shape of a roulette wheel, but there was no light in the room. Presumably, nobody played before dinner. From a room on the left came the chink of billiard balls. Bond looked around and found himself alone in the corridor. He knocked discreetly on the door and turned the handle.

A man with his back to Bond was lining up a shot. Three Egyptian girls of exceptional but rather flashy loveliness were lounging around the room in long evening dresses. They looked like bored fashion models waiting for the photographer to finish loading his Pentax. With Bond's appearance they became sufficiently animated to sniff the air for the scent of money, but when they found there was none they went back to looking bored. One of the girls was holding a cigar, the second the cue chalk, and the third had nothing to keep herself amused. The air was heavy with cigar smoke and Guerlain's Ode. Bond waited for the man to play his shot and then cleared his throat.

"Mr. Kalba?"

The man did not look directly at Bond but walked around the table and took the chalk from one of the girls. He was wearing an over-padded dinner jacket that looked like armor-plating, and his short, fat fingers glittered with diamonds. They were not, thought Bond, hands that deserved any ornament, let alone anything so vulgarly meretricious. The face with its narrow, wary eyes and Mr. Punch nose was cruel and swarthy and the flesh scuffed and pockmarked like the outside of a much-played golf-ball. Despite its limitations as a work of art, the face commanded respect. It was arrogant, perhaps too arrogant for its own good, and ruthless in a way that suggested it had found being ruthless pays.

"Who wants him?"

The man did not wait for an answer to his question but handed back the chalk and leaned over the table. The cue came back swiftly and decisively and then shot forward. It was a difficult shot. The cue ball played flat and hard without spin to kiss the red and then come back with sufficient momentum off the end cushion to touch the side of the table and then drift back endlessly toward the lonely white ball six inches from the near cushion. Kalba took his eye off the cue ball when it was halfway down the table on its return journey and reached for his cigar. He did not need to look. He knew the ball was going to find its target.

"My name is Bond. James Bond."

"What of it?" The reply was contemptuous, and Kalba prepared to play another shot. The expression on the girls' faces was now one of disapproval.

"You had an appointment with Mr. Fekkesh."

The silence in the room had the sharp edge of tension. Kalba stopped in his preparation and straightened up. He faced Bond and for the first time looked directly into his eyes. Bond felt as if the man was prising away flesh and bone to get inside his brain. "Well?" The word was a pistol shot.

"You won't be seeing him for a long time."

"What do you mean?" Kalba's hand tightened around the cue.

"He's dead."

Kalba turned to the girls and jerked his head toward the door. Without demur they started to file out, leaving behind the chalk and the cigar. "Why do you bring me this news?"

"Because I believe you have something to sell, and I'm interested in buying."

"And so am I."

Bond spun around to find Anya standing behind him. There was a grim, determined line to her jaw. His heart sank. Blast the woman! He didn't seem to be able to make a move without her dogging his footsteps. Was she alone, or were there two more goons waiting outside the door?

Kalba looked from one face to the other. "Well, well. How interesting. It is obvious that you two are not colleagues. I suppose some kind of auction would be the most sensible way in which to proceed." The old arrogance had returned. In another moment he would start playing billiards again. "I wonder if you will be able to match this lady's figure, Mr. Bond."

Kalba was enjoying his joke when the door opened. Bond tensed for action, but it was one of the club servants. He looked at Bond and Anya suspiciously before turning to Kalba. "Sir, you are required urgently on the telephone."

Kalba's face showed irritation. "Have it transferred here, you fool!"

"Sir, that is impossible. The call has come through on the outside line in the telephone room."

Kalba sucked in his breath and turned to Bond and Anya. "Perhaps a welcome respite. It will give you time to discuss your opening bids."

Bond held up a restraining hand. "Before there's any question of opening bids, I'd like to be certain there's something to bid for."

Kalba smiled. "Oh, yes. There's something to bid for all

87

right." His mole hand burrowed into an inside pocket and emerged with a small metal canister. "I keep it here. Close to my heart." Kalba opened his jacket to reveal the Browning strapped beneath his left armpit. He showed his teeth once more and dropped the canister back into his pocket. Bond debated whether to make a lightning attack and decided against it. With Kalba by himself he would have stood a chance but the henchman was watching him like a hawk and had a menacing bulge beneath his armpit which was probably not caused by weight-lifting. He stood to one side deferentially and Kalba left the room. The door closed. Bond turned and looked purposefully into Anya's challenging blue eyes. "Now tell me. Just what is happening?"

Max Kalba did not rub his hands together as he walked briskly toward the telephone room, but anyone watching his progress would have been able to tell that he was pleased. And why not? Two rich customers had arrived in person to do business, and their rivalry could only force up the price of the merchandise. Whichever of them had put paid to Fekkish had only saved him the trouble of performing an act which would have to have been done sooner or later. It was not just a question of the money. There was going to be more than enough even for him. It was making sure that Stromberg never caught up with him. When he changed his face and went to live in South America, he did not want to leave anyone who would be in a position to betray him. Even the source of all the wealth to come, Stromberg's beautiful but treacherous assistant was going to get a nasty surprise when the time came for her to suddenly leave her employer and fly to join him. Kalba smiled grimly and pushed open the door of the telephone room.

A repairman in khaki work clothes was squatting with his back to the door; Kalba glimpsed an open tin box containing tools. He moved toward the booth in which the receiver was dangling. It was only as he was passing the man that he suddenly felt the room growing cold. It was as if he had stepped into a refrigerator. But the cold was not in the air. It was in his instinctive presentiment of danger. He started to turn, but his hand never got farther than the inside of his jacket. Huge fingers closed about the base of his neck and propelled him forward into the box until his face slammed with sickening force against the far wall. He felt his nose break with the impact and his mouth filled with blood. Still the hand did not release its grip but turned his head with a wrench that nearly tore it from its socket. The enormous, lumpish face was an inch away. Greaseballs of sweat glistened from the honeycomb of open pores. The tiny pig eyes glinted evilly. Kalba tried to scream, but no sound came.

Jaws thrust him back into the corner and bared his teeth.

Chapter 12

A CLASH OF PERSONALITIES

Bond looked down into the beautiful blue eyes staring up at him brazenly. Could she be telling the truth? The Russians did not own the tracking system. They had responded to the same invitation to do business as the British. That would explain why they had thought he killed Fekkesh. And if the defector was not Russian, he must have been working for someone else. Someone else who had developed the tracking system. Someone else who was now working with ruthless determination to recover his property. And the big animal with the teeth. He must be working for them. He had eliminated Fekkesh and now, who was next in line? Bond immediately felt uneasy. Kalba's telephone call was taking a long time. He nodded to Anya. "You will have to excuse me for a few moments. Don't start negotiations without me."

He left the room under her scornful gaze and strode toward the telephone with a sense of impending disaster. Dark almond eyes in the bar darted toward him longingly, but he was unaware of their attention. He crossed the entrance hall and threw open the door of the telephone room. A window was open and a curtain stirred in the breeze. One booth was open and empty, one shut with an "Out of order" notice on it. With a terrible foreboding, Bond opened the door and a bloodstained heap of still-warm flesh crumpled at his feet. He looked down at the gaping neck and again fought a desire to be sick. He was no stranger to death, but this was an obscenity. Conquering his loathing, he dropped to his knees and turned the body over. A quick search revealed that the microfilm and the Browning had gone.

Bond crossed to the window and judged the distance to the ground. Six feet. He swung his legs over the sill and dropped to land in the gravel with his arms spread wide. There was no sound. Just lines of expensive motorcars gleaming in the darkness. He advanced to the first clump of palms and listened. Had the man again disappeared into thin air? Then there was a stab of light, and Bond saw a heavy silhouette levering itself into the front of a small truck. The door slammed and the light disappeared.

Bond doubled around in a semicircle and came up behind the vehicle as the starter began to hector life into the engine. If only he had the Walther! There was no possibility of his being able to tackle this armed ogre with his bare hands. The engine still refused to fire and Bond closed with the back of the truck and pressed down the handle. One of the doors swung open and he quickly scrambled inside amongst a welter of cables, wires, and junction boxes. Now the engine exploded into resentful life and the truck began to tremble. Bond held his breath and waited for it to move forward.

Then the back door opened.

Bond's heart jumped to his mouth before he recognized Anya scrambling in beside him. In her hand was a Beretta .25 levelled at a point equidistant between his eyes. A Beretta .25. His old gun. The gun he had carried for fifteen years until it failed him once and was sentenced to death by a Court of Inquiry and the evidence of Major Boothroyd, Armourer to International Export and the world's greatest small arms expert.

Bond looked from the weapon to Anya with cold ironic eyes. "If we go on meeting like this, people will start to talk."

Anya moved the gun close to Bond's heart and spoke in a low whisper. "What happened to Kalba?"

"He's dead."

"And the microfilm?"

Bond jerked his head toward the front of the truck. Anya followed his glance warily and then slid a slim hand inside his jacket. Bond smiled cynically. "And I thought Russian women were incapable of feeling."

Undeterred, Anya continued to frisk him. "Make no mistake, Commander. I intend to recover that microfilm."

"Exactly my own sentiment. That's why I'm sitting in this rather uncomfortable truck." Bond nodded toward the Beretta. "Do put that thing away. You're not going to fire it and let our friend know we're here."

In the cab, Jaws listened to Bond's words floating up from the small speaker set into the dashboard and furled his lips back in a metallic smile. Stromberg would be pleased with him. As instructed, he had eliminated the two traitors and now, as a bonus, he was going to remove two other sources of potential nuisance to the organization. Jaws spread his elbows and draped himself over the wheel in preparation for a long drive.

Jaws' real name was Zbigniew Krycsiwiki. He was born in Poland, the product of a union between the strong man of a travelling circus and the Chief Wardress at the Women's Prison at Kracow. The relationship and subsequent marriage was a stormy one and, when it broke up, the young Zbigniew stayed with his mother and attended school and subsequently university at Kracow. He grew to a prodigious height but in temperament he followed his father and was surly and uncooperative, given to sudden outbreaks of violent temper. Because of his size he commanded a place on the university basketball team, but he was sluggish of reaction and his lack of speed was constantly exposed by more skillful but less physically endowed players. This lack of ability to compete despite his natural advantages preyed upon his mind and he became, more and more, a dirty player signalled out by the crowd for jeers and abuse. A series of incidents culminated in his being ordered from the court during a key match against Posnan and reaching up to tear down the net and assault the referee. A merciless flaying with the loop of metal meant that the official had his scalp lifted from his head before Zbigniew was eventually pacified.

That was the end of his career as a basketball player and university student. He worked for a while for a butcher and then in a slaughter house before being arrested by the secret police in the 1972 bread riots. His appearance on the streets hurling paving stones owed nothing to political conviction but was a direct result of his natural appetite for violence. This appetite was temporarily sated when the police manacled his hands behind his back in a punishment cell and beat him with hollow steel clubs encased in thick leather until his jaw was turned into bone meal. They left him, thinking they had killed him, but they reckoned without the tenacious hold on life exerted by Zbigniew Krycsiwiki. He pried the cuff of one of the manacles apart on a wall hook, strangled a warder, and drove through the prison gates—and three guards who got in his way—in a stolen three-ton truck. He exchanged this for a private car and drove to Gdansk where he succeeded in stowing away on one of the Stromberg's vessels that happened to be taking on timber in the port.

He was eventually discovered near to death as the vessel neared Malmo. Reports of his grotesque size and appearance attracted the interest of Stromberg, who flew down from Stockholm to view the strange stowaway. To Stromberg, ugliness could be more affecting than beauty, and in Zbigniew's swollen, brutish face and huge, ungainly body he saw a creature that might have come from the stygian, unexplored depths of the ocean. He determined to recast him in the mold of his imagination and when told by local medical opinion that the jaw could never be rebuilt, he cast farther afield.

Doctor Ludwig Schwenk had been responsible for many

of the more notorious experiments on human guinea pigs, in Buchenwald. He had grafted an Alsatian's head to a man's body and kept the resulting mutation alive for three weeks. He had experimented with genital transplants, some of them involving animals. With the collapse of Nazi Germany he had fled to Sweden, changed his name, and set up practice as a country G.P. in a village near Halmstad. Part of Stromberg's income accrued from blackmailing Nazi war criminals with the threat of revealing their whereabouts to agents of the Israeli Mossad. It was a simple matter to persuade Schwenk to take an interest in Zbigniew's case. After fourteen operations involving the grafting of tissue and the insertion of platinized steel components, the artificial jaw was operational. Only one sacrifice was necessary. In order to work the jaw, Zbigniew's vocal cords had to be severed and reharnessed to the electric impulse conductor that opened and shut the two rows of terrifying, razor-sharp teeth. Zbigniew Krycsiwiki was now mute. Like a fish.

It was six o'clock when the jolt of the vehicle coming to a halt made Bond open his eyes. He was cold and stiff, and Anya was leaning against his chest, asleep. Her shoulders were slightly hunched as if she sought to nuzzle closer to whatever warmth his body might provide. Bond shook her gently awake and saw her eyes suddenly open wide like those of a startled animal. She turned her head and, seeing what she had been using as a pillow, drew quickly away.

The cab door slammed and Bond tensed, ready to spring if the back of the van opened. Beside him, Anya retrieved the Beretta from a side pocket of her evening bag and trained it on the doors. Seconds passed. Bond edged forward and slowly pushed one of the doors until there was a quarter-inch gap. Sand and a sandstone wall about three feet away. He pushed the door wider and waited. Nothing happened. The wall rose to about twenty feet and was surmounted by a carved lion, its features worn away by millenia of desert sandstorms. Bond swung his stiff legs over the back of the van and dropped noiselessly to the sand. He squatted down and peered under the wheels. There was no sign of anyone. Only a huge jumble of masonry giving the impression of a box of children's building bricks scattered across the sand. Giant columns, ornamental façades, avenues, esplanades, and doorways, triumphal arches, rows of sphinxes and huge statues with their faces eaten away by time and the elements.

"Where are we?" Anya was at his side.

"I don't know. Some kind of ancient city." Bond gazed around. The sand stretched away on all sides. "Wait here." Her eyes blazed, but she stayed where she was while he edged forward and peered into the driver's cab through the open window. It was empty. He returned to her side. "Right. We've got to find him." He glanced at the Beretta. "Do you know how to use that thing?"

She looked at him with proud contempt. "You will see."

Damn you, thought Bond. How many women do I know who could look so overwhelmingly beautiful after being cooped up in the back of a van for the night? I don't want to compete with you, I want to make love to you. "Don't forget," he said gruffly, trying to get a grip on his feelings. "When we catch up with our friend, it's every man for himself."

"And every woman." Anya threw back her head defiantly.

"Do you want me to lead?"

Bond allowed the slim line of her body to pass ahead and resisted the temptation to kick her in the middle of her beautifully shaped behind.

The first rays of the sun shone directly in their faces as they skirted the avenue of sphinxes and moved warily through an opening in a high wall and into an inner courtyard containing two rows of stone columns rising to a height of sixty feet. Bond looked about him and felt uneasy. Anybody lying in wait for them would have an overwhelming advantage. Why had the executioner come here? Was he looking for something? Was he meeting someone?

Anya moved gracefully from pillar to pillar. Bond slapped viciously at the first fly of the day and sent his eyes scaling the jagged mountains of stone. This part must have been some kind of temple. And now they were approaching a second courtyard where restoration work was in hand. An untidy framework of scaffolding lay against a great stone façade carved into the relief of a pharaoh. There was a pulley for raising stones and every floor of the scaffolding was littered with pieces of masonry. There was no sign of workmen. One arm of the pharaoh was lifted dramatically, and between his spread legs was the entrance to a tunnel. Anya looked toward the tunnel and nodded. Bond threw a finger forward in a gesture of acquiescence and then took her by the arm and led her around the perimeter of the courtyard. There was something about this place that gave him the heebie-jeebies. It was like the props room of a folded theatrical company. No sun peered into the courtyard, and the gloomy pharaoh seemed to be raising his fist against the high walls that pressed in on him, as if daring them to come any closer. Bond looked at the giant stone fist silhouetted against the blue sky and marvelled that the heat haze could start so early. The stone actually seemed to be trembling.

And then he realized that it *was* trembling.

Not only trembling, but tipping forward. With a shout, he hurled Anya to one side and threw himself backwards against the nearest wall. Two tons of granite hissed into the sand between them, and the ground shook. Bond licked his dry lips and looked up. Jaws was standing on the edge of the topmost platform of the still-shaking scaffolding. A guttural grunt broke from the back of his throat and he threw himself at the hook of the pulley. With a banshee scream the rope snaked out and the huge man hurtled down to land in front of Bond with an impact scarcely less startling than that of the block of masonry.

Bond prepared to defend himself, but his heart quailed. Even without the terrifying teeth the man was awesome. Bond was over six feet tall, but he would have to grow another fourteen inches to match this giant. His arms were like weightlifters' legs, and his extended fingers could have touched three sides of a chessboard. As Bond took up his fighting crouch, the man's head tilted back and the lips parted slowly. The unveiling of the hideous, jagged teeth was calculated to strike fear, like the raising of the dorsal spines of a fighting fish.

Bond circled warily. What was Anya doing with her gun? Was she going to wait for him to be killed? Jaws's arm rose slowly like the arm of a crane, and a great hand closed about the heavy metal hook of the block and tackle. Bond saw the glint in the eye and felt like a coconut in a coconut shy. "Yuh!" The huge arm flexed and enough metal to forge an anvil screamed toward Bond. He hurled himself to one side and the rope stung him like a whiplash as it whistled past. Behind him there was a sound like the aftermath of a demolition gang swinging an iron ball at a building. Jaws smiled and lumbered forward. Bond ducked inside the groping arms and aimed a right cross at the heavy jaw. It was a perfect punch. He knew it the moment his arm swung away from his body. And then the impact. Flesh and bone against solid metal. It was like punching the side of a tank. For a moment he thought he had shattered his knuckle. A flame of pain ran up his arm to the socket. Jaws's hands fell on his shoulders like meal sacks and hurled him back into the scaffolding. The back of his head struck a metal upright, and his spine felt as if it had been driven against his rib cage. He was on fire with pain, the wind driven from his body. Desperately trying to raise his arms, he felt himself sliding toward the ground. Jaws moved forward for the *coup de grâce*, his steel teeth parting like the expectant maw of a guillotine.

"Stay where you are!"

Bond turned his dazed head to see Anya, her gun trained unflinchingly on Jaws. Jaws peered down on it as if it was some malevolent insect.

"The microfilm. Throw it at my feet!"

Jaws hesitated and then slowly introduced a hand into one of his pockets. Bond fought to clear his head and get the breath circulating through his aching body. He could feel the flies crawling over his bleeding knuckle. Jaws withdrew his hand and lobbed the small canister at Anya's feet. Anya bent down and at that instant Jaws lashed out with his foot, kicking sand into her face. She fired blind and missed. Jaws kicked again, and the gun sailed into the scaffolding. Bond dived for it and again was seized by Jaws, who threw him like a bundle of laundry into the thicket of metal. He dragged himself to his knees and saw Jaws coming for him with a short length of scaffolding, wielding it like a baseball bat. "Yuh!" The shoulders came back and the biceps locked. There was a hiss of air, and Bond ducked as the steel club whistled toward his head.

With a hideous, teeth-grating screech it exploded against an upright and knocked it two feet out of true. A cloud of dust and stones poured down, and the scaffolding squeaked and trembled. Bond, sprawled on his back, turned on his side in a desperate attempt to rise. His spine throbbed and every movement sent sharp daggers of pain stabbing through his body. Jaws had raised the piece of piping above his head and was stepping forward. Bond scrambled back on his elbows and felt the wall block his retreat. There was no escape. Bond could feel the fear rushing through him like a spring tide. He looked about him, hoping to light on some weapon. There was nothing. Jaws's eyes were now tiny laser beams of concentration. He was bent on extermination, not amusement. Bond saw the crooked upright and knew it was his only chance. Summoning up all his strength, he drew back both feet and lashed out. The soles and heels of his shoes landed solidly and together, and the upright was knocked sideways.

There was a crack like a stick snapping and Bond rolled sideways waiting for the impact of the blow that was going to shatter his head like a pineapple. It did not come. Instead, there was a mounting rumble, building into a roar. The whole structure around him began to crumble, and a block of stone crashed down inches from his fingers. The scaffolding was breaking up like a dynamited log jam. Dust and rubble poured down and a falling plank brushed his shoulder. Bond rolled again and then half scrambled, half ran, expecting at any second to be crushed to death as he fled into the courtyard. He ran until the roar no longer seemed to pursue him and then collapsed on his knees. Behind him the last plank tipped, teetered, and fell, and the dust began to settle.

Three-quarters of the scaffolding had collapsed and there was now an untidy heap of stones and timber rising to the pharaoh's knees. Of Anya and the man with the

98

metal mouth, there was no sign. Bond rubbed some of the dust from his face and fought away the flies. The man must be dead, crushed under the stones. But Anya? Bond moved forward and surveyed the sand around the scaffolding. There was no sign of the metal canister. He turned and drove his weary limbs toward the van. If she had the microfilm, that was where she would head.

He ran through the columns, screwing up his eyes against the pain. His back felt as if it was broken. The sun dazzled him. Through the hole in the wall and along the avenue of sphinxes. Bond came up behind the passenger side of the van because there was less chance of being seen in a rear-view mirror and raised his hand to grip the door handle. A pause, and he hauled it open. Anya was bent over the controls, fiddling with a couple of wires under the dashboard. The canister and the Beretta lay on the seat beside her. Bond lunged for them gratefully and slipped them in his pocket. "I didn't know you were mechanically minded." He held out the ignition key. "Why don't you try this? You'll find it easier."

With a noise like a bomb dropping, Jaws landed on the hood in front of them. He had jumped twelve feet from the wall. The hood buckled, and Jaws's head butted the windshield, sending out a radiating spider's web of cracks. His face was bleeding through the dust, and his eyes were insane.

"Step on it!" Bond relinquished the key and reached for the Beretta. As the engine leaped into life, Jaws rolled from the hood and snatched at the handle of Bond's door. Bond locked it half a second before the fist formed around the metal and the handle was torn off. Anya fought the wheel around and the van leaped forward. Like a wounded buffalo, Jaws charged the vehicle and butted and kicked it. There was no easy escape route from the ruin. Anya had to reverse. She clawed at the wheel and accelerated backwards. Jaws threw his bulk to one side and the van crashed against the wall. He hurled himself forward and, tearing off a bumper, used it as a flail to belabor the box on wheels that was enraging him. It was how he had attacked the referee at the basketball match. Anya swung the van around, but the lock was not tight enough. A block of stone barred their escape. Again she reversed, and Bond momentarily lost sight of the mad giant.

When he turned his head it was to see the great open mouth clamped around the molded metal that divided the windshield from Anya's door frame. He was trying to bite his way into the truck! Bond felt his foot pressing down against the floor as he urged the vehicle forward. He heard the wheels spinning in the deep sand, and fresh terror surged through him. Anya was biting her lips as she tried to concentrate on the engine revs. The metal of the frame was starting to buckle . . . Bond reached across Anya and fired at point-blank range. There was a crash, a spark, and a wild, humming whine. The bullet had ricocheted off the steel teeth. The huge head jerked back like a buffer and the wheels at last gripped the sand. The van lurched out of the trough it had dug for itself and began to gather speed. The coachwork groaned, creaked, and rasped, but there were no longer any sounds of attack. Bond expelled a deep sigh of relief and looked in the side mirror. The man was standing, immobile and still threatening, looking after them. Seen against the background of the ruin, he seemed to belong to it, like Frankenstein's monster to some turreted, vampire-haunted castle.

Bond returned the Beretta to his pocket nearest the window and wondered what words were appropriate at such moments of deliverance. Anya had stopped biting her lips, but there was still the same expression of grim determination. "Thanks for leaving me alone with Prince Charming," he said.

Anya shrugged. "Every man and woman for himself. Remember?"

"Still, I suppose you did intervene at a propitious moment earlier on."

Anya wrinkled her delicious nose. "We all make mistakes." Bond smiled and watched the track stretching away before them. With any luck he could be back in Cairo by the evening. And then? Probably best to get around to the fall-back address he had been given and hand over the merchandise. Not a good idea to keep it in a hotel room.

He glanced toward Anya. The lay could make her own arrangements.

Bond slipped his hand into his pocket and removed the canister. He expected a reaction from Anya, but there was none. She continued to look steadfastly ahead, both hands on the wheel in the ten to three position approved by the British School of Motoring. Bond unscrewed the canister and tapped out the thin spool of film. A couple of inches of celluloid that could change the history of the world. How unreal it all seemed. He raised the film to the light and studied it. Anya changed gear and did not return her hand to the driving wheel. From the corner of his eye, Bond noticed it missing and glanced down. The slim hand nestled in a position of intimacy against his thigh. Bond looked toward Anya and she turned her face to his. The chin tilted and the beautiful eyes were full of bland innocence. Bland innocence laced with triumph.

Bond's hand dived toward his thigh, but it was too late. A wasp had stung him. Already its poison coursed through his veins like numbing fire. He could feel his neck stiffening, his fingers locking. The film dropped to the floor. Against his leg, the needle still glinted evilly from the center of the ring. How stupid of him. How typical of SMERSH. Have you so short a memory, James Bond? Do you not remember Rosa Klebb? Now he could feel nothing, and the puppet strings that pulled his mind were being snipped one by one. There was only the soft female voice whispering to him like a chiding lover.

"Remember, dear James Bond. Every woman for herself."

Chapter 13

A MARRIAGE OF CONVENIENCE

James Bond walked through the teeming Khalili bazaar and felt a weariness near to death. Whatever poison the Russian bitch had pumped into him—and Bond favored a relation of curare with its hatchet effect on the central nervous system—was still creeping through him like an anesthetist in carpet slippers, and there was no part of his bruised tortured body that did not ache. But the ache that really counted was deep inside. Beyond reach of the most powerful electric current.

It was the ache of failure.

Bond was not used to crawling back with his tail between his legs, and he did not relish the prospect of arriving at Station Y with nothing to show for his efforts but multiple contusions and a hideous, nagging fear that he might now be impotent.

"This way, sah! This way! You want beautiful gold thing for your lady? We have it. I give you special price."

"Look, look! I show you. Come, come. This real silver. Very old. I show you mark."

"You Engleesh? I like Engleesh! Engleesh very good friend of mine. I fight for Engleesh army. Because you Engleesh I show you leather work I never sell. It come down from my father. He also like Engleesh very much—"

Bond felt like a man swimming against the tide. If anyone tried to sell him dirty postcards he might go under. And then he saw what he was looking for. "Khan Carpets. Tapis Khan." A tall Arab caught his eye and swept toward him.

"Good day, sir! We have the finest selection of carpets in Cairo."

"I am only interested in Persian carpets."

"Then we will be able to give you satisfaction, sir. If you come inside . . ."

Bond listened to the exchange of recognition signals and felt that it sounded like a music-hall act. Perhaps it was because he was bruised in mind and body and not looking forward to his next appointment. "007's on the slide, you know. Made a pig's ear of some caper in Egypt. Little Russky filly took him to the cleaners. Lucky to get away without a Court of Inquiry. I think they're going to find him a staff job." He could hear the tittle-tattle reverberating around International Export. Oh well, what the hell. He'd had a good inning. But if he ever caught up with Major Anya Amasova again, she'd have a darn sight more than a tanned bottom to remember him by!

The dark, cool interior of the shop was like a labyrinth, with passages leading off in all directions. It was also open to another narrow, bustling street at the back. Very useful for comings and goings if one was being followed. The guide stopped in a small room that could be entered by either of two doors. The walls were hung with carpets. Bond noticed the Arab's eyes darting around suspiciously before he spoke. "I think you will find that this is what you are looking for, sir."

He swiftly pulled aside a carpet and ushered Bond through the opening that was revealed. Bond nodded and passed into a narrow corridor. A second after the carpet had fallen behind him, a light came on. The smell was like that of a house that has been closed for the winter: people pickled in cold and damp. Bond followed the corridor and came to a flight of stone steps. As he started to descend he heard a familiar sound—the tip-tapping of a typewriter.

What he saw as he came into the low-vaulted room was no less familiar. Sitting behind a desk was the secretary he had last seen in M's outer office. She had a cardigan pulled around her shoulders and was leaning across the typewriter with a correcting eraser between her teeth. She finished adjusting the machine and made a shivering gesture. "Chilly, isn't it?" Bond nodded. "I think it'll be all right if you go in." She turned her head toward the door behind her and set to work briskly with the eraser. Bond took hold of himself and stepped forward. What the devil was going on?

He opened the door and found himself in a long white-washed room, mercifully warmer than its antechamber—secretaries always had to suffer; that was one of the rules of the Civil Service. At the end of the room was a wide, polished wood desk with four wire baskets on it and behind the desk—a woman in the uniform of a Russian Army Major training a Walther PPK on him. Anya! Her eyes narrowed as he came in, and her elbow advanced across the desk. The barrel was pointing at his heart. Was he going mad?

While Bond blinked and stared and wondered if he was going to be shot dead or come to his senses, another actor entered the drama. He was dressed in the uniform of a Colonel-General in the Russian Army and he had three rows of ribbons on his chest. Bond recognized him from his photographs. Colonel-General Nikitin, head of SMERSH. He looked at Bond and then back through the door by which he had entered the room.

The next entrant made Bond certain that soon men in white tunics would be leading him away to what was discreetly known as the service's Rest and Recuperation Center at Virginia Water. M, sucking on his pipe and sporting one of his infernally cheerful bow ties. He jabbed the stem of his pipe at Bond in greeting and moved behind the desk as Anya stood up.

"Ah, 007. You're here."

Anya turned the Walther around so that she was holding it by the barrel and advanced to Bond. Her smile was charming. "I seem to have managed to lay hands on your gun—as well as other things." Bond took the proffered weapon and resisted the temptation to test-fire it immediately. He turned to M. "I'm afraid I don't understand, sir."

M waved everybody to seats. "There's been a change of plan, 007. General Nikitin and his A.D.C., Major Amasova, are officially here as part of the delegation discussing defense matters with President Sadat. That doesn't concern us—well, it does, but it doesn't, if you know what I mean." Bond nodded briskly. He was not in the mood for M's light-heartedness. "Their real business is rather more serious and immediate. You may not be aware of it, but the Russians have also lost a nuclear submarine."

Bond's pulse quickened. He had not known. He looked toward Anya, who gazed at him without expression. Only a slight widening of her eyes seemed to say, "Could you be so naive as to expect me to tell you all my secrets?"

"To cut a long story short, our governments have decided, at the highest level, that our mutual interests would be best served if we worked together on this assignment. We have no knowledge as to who is responsible for the disappearance of our submarines, and exhaustive inquiries amongst Allies have revealed nothing. We are up against a completely unknown entity."

"I see." Bond thought of the two men who had fastened the electrodes to his genitals. They would be his allies if they were still alive. Such opportunities for discovering new friends made the whole job seem worthwhile.

Nikitin leaned toward Anya and spoke in Russian. His message completed, he sat back and smiled at Bond. The only sincere thing about the smile was that it revealed he wore false teeth and rarely bothered to clean them. In terms of genuine warmth it carried the same weight of feeling as the polar ice cap. The mouth moved, but the eyes levelled like the barrels of a twelve-bore.

Anya became her master's voice. "Comrade General states that we have entered into a new era of Anglo-Soviet cooperation. That is why, as a symbol of Russian good faith, he has made available the microfilm recovered from sources that I need hardly bother to remind you of, Commander Bond?"

Bond inclined his head with all the grace that he could muster and then straightened up. "I would also like to proffer another reason."

M took his pipe from his mouth. "Which is?"

"On first examination, the microfilm appears to be useless, sir."

A glacial silence fell on the room warmed only by the glow from M's pipe. "Continue, 007."

"Well, sir. When I looked at the microfilm there appeared to be some tiny scratches on it. They suggested to me that key technical data on the blueprint had been scrubbed out. I'd say that the microfilm is merely intended to show that whoever we're dealing with really does have the goods. In other words, as it stands, it's of no use to anyone"—Bond returned Nikitin's smile—"except, of course, as a gift."

The two off-white worms that were Nikitin's lips closed over the yellow teeth and the artificial fire behind the eyes was switched off with a click.

"Interesting." M turned from the silent Nikitin with the suspicion of a raised eyebrow. "In a moment we'll have the chance to see if your conjecture is correct, 007. I've asked for the microfilm to be put on the Magnoscope." M flicked a switch on his intercom. "All right, Belling. We're ready when you are."

"Very good, sir."

The lights in the room were lowered and a large screen slowly descended from the ceiling. A panel of light in the wall behind M's desk showed where the projection room was located. Bond concentrated on the screen and felt the palms of his hands growing damp. He was going to look a damn fool if his supposition was proved wrong. The screen filled with symbols that Bond could easily have mistaken for the Dead Sea Scrolls. To his relief, he noted that there were several places where it looked as though material had been clumsily blotted out.

M spoke into the intercom. "Well, Belling. What can

you tell us?" The earnest, intense, grammar-school voice came back almost immediately. Bond could almost see the man straining toward the microphone. "Well, sir. It's good stuff as far as it goes. All the data seem,—er, very genuine. Trouble is, it's missing out the vital bits. There's nothing there we don't know already. It whets the appetite, though."

Bond peered at the seemingly incomprehensible jumble of figures and symbols. "Is there anything to suggest where the blueprint was drafted?"

"I was just going to come to that." Belling sounded slightly peeved by the interruption. "We think it might have been done in Italy. The size is in pro to Venetian Octavo and the script has an Italianate flavor to it. There's a slight upward stress on the transversals."

"Is it not possible to get the definition better?" asked Anya.

"I'm afraid not, miss. Whoever shot this microfilm didn't take a lot of care about it. The lighting is very bad. You can't blow up what's not there in the first place."

"If it's been done badly, it's probably because it had to be done quickly," said M. "It fits in with our impression that somebody was indulging in what might be described as industrial espionage." Bond leaned toward the screen. Was that a smudge in the bottom right-hand corner, or could he make out the very, very faint outline of lettering? He walked toward the screen and pointed.

"Could you enlarge this section, please?"

"Try for you, sir. Can't guarantee you'll see much."

The screen went blank and then flashed a series of giant close-ups as the projectionist homed in on the wanted segment. Bond glanced toward Anya. She was gazing raptly at the screen, her chin tilted forward on the heel of her hand. She looked like a keen student attending her first lecture. There was something natural and unforced about her pose that was beguiling. She was a strange girl. There was not that coldness and remoteness that permeated most of the Russian spies he had come across.

Nikitin saw Bond glance at Anya and felt the cold snake of jealousy crawl across his belly. Bond's appetite for women was well known to SMERSH and had twice nearly been his downfall. Perhaps, on this occasion, it would be third time lucky. It would be interesting to see Anya's reaction when she learned that Bond had murdered her lover. He would continue to conceal the news for now but, later on in the operation, it might be advisable, from all points of view, to tell her the truth. When a sound lead was established on the tracking system Bond would immediately become expendable. Anya could eliminate him and then, and then—Nikitin thought of the films of Anya's love-making that had been sent to him from the Black Sea course and stewed the thin gruel of saliva behind his death-mask lips. What delicious possibilities existed! He would harness himself to her and drive her like a Cossack. And while he rode the soft, white flesh he would think of the hated British spy she had killed. It would be almost as perfect as having Bond to himself, strapped face downward on the interrogation table beneath the palace of death that was No. 13, Sretenka Ulitsa . . .

"Hold it there!" Bond felt a sense of mounting excitement as he looked at the screen. There was a diagonal line running from top to bottom which marked the edge of the blueprint, and on its right some shadowy lettering lacking the blunted hardness of the symbols on the blueprint. When the blueprint was photographed, it must have been lying on something and that something had crept into the right-hand corner of the microfilm. Bond strained to read the lettering. O-R-A-T-O-R-Y. There was also a symbol.

"Oratory." M read the word out. "What do you make of that, Belling?"

"I don't know, sir. It looks like the right-hand corner of a letterhead. You can see the outline of the paper. The blueprint must have been resting on it when it was photographed." Bond was glad to hear his hypothesis confirmed. "An oratory is a small chapel, usually a private one. Used to be the name of a small Catholic public school, as well."

"They must have had a remarkably advanced science sixth if they were inventing submarine tracking systems," said M drily. "I know the Jesuits are reputed to be damn clever but—" He shrugged and turned toward Anya who was biting a lip as she stared at the screen.

108

"I have seen that symbol," she said. The light of battle shone in her eyes.

"Looks like a bishop's miter, sir." That was Belling's contribution.

M snorted. "Perhaps we should make some discreet inquiries at the Vatican."

Bond screwed up his eyes. The girl was right. The symbol was, if not familiar, one he had seen before somewhere. Two upright, overlapping ovals, the uppermost with a notch, standing on a truncated isosceles triangle. The whole traversed by rows of zigzag lines. What did it remind him of?

"Or a fish, sir," said Belling.

Anya slapped her hand down on the table. "Stromberg! That is the symbol of the Stromberg Shipping Line."

Of course! Bond kicked himself for not getting there first. Sigmund Stromberg. A man who had come from nowhere to build up a huge merchant fleet in a matter of years; one of the first to see the commercial advantages of moving huge quantities of oil in super-tankers and now owner of four of them with an individual dead weight in excess of four hundred and fifty thousand tons. A man who was reputed to be ruthless in his business dealings and suspected of involvement in the recent spate of tankers that had broken up in American waters—all of them belonging to rival operators. The Stromberg symbol was a squat fish standing on its tail.

"Well done." Bond extended grudging congratulations like the losing captain in a prep school rugby match.

"Interesting," mused M. "But what about this 'Oratory'? Does he support any religious foundations?"

Anya's nostrils flared. "Like a good capitalist, he supports only himself."

Bond tried to concentrate. Oratory, oratory. What the devil did it mean? Anya was right. Stromberg had never shown any signs of altruism or desire to become a philanthropist. Unless one counted his reported interest in oceanography. Bond remembered reading something about Stromberg's setting up a Marine Research Laboratory in

the Mediterranean. That was probably as near as he—
Eureka!

"Laboratory!" Bond almost shouted the word. "Not 'Oratory'—Laboratory! The first syllable was obscured by the blueprint. Stromberg has a marine research laboratory somewhere. Corsica, I think."

"Sardinia," said Anya shortly. She hesitated and then a tremulous half-smile spread across her lovely, tilting lips as she looked at Bond. "Well done."

"Ye-es," said M, looking from Bond to Anya before turning toward Nikitin. "Well done, indeed. Gratifying to discover this new era of Anglo-Soviet cooperation of which you spoke so heart-rendingly bearing fruit in such a short time." He tapped burning shards of tobacco from his upturned pipe into a large stone ashtray. "It augurs well for the future."

Nikitin nodded slowly, his eyes meting out death sentences. M turned back to Bond and Anya. "I suggest you proceed to Sardinia or Corsica, or wherever Stromberg's marine laboratory · is located, with all possible speed."

Bond drew away from the challenging lapis lazuli of Anya's eyes. "In what capacity, sir?"

M tapped his pipe like an auctioneer bringing down his gavel for the final time. "Well, all things considered, there seems to be only one capacity—that of man and wife."

Chapter 14

THE DROWNED VOLCANO

Anya's blind fingers traced a path across the rough, hot stone and closed about the supple plastic. Its tapered haft settled into the palm of the hand and her thumb and first finger tightened against the minuscule serrations on the cap. An anticlockwise twist and the thumb flicked languidly until the cap dropped to the stone with a sound that wobbled into silence. With eyes still closed, she slid her left hand forward and pressed the nose of the Piz-bruin against its palm. Pressure from three fingers and the tube gave a small, sibilant hiss and relinquished a teaspoonful of warm, liquid cream. Anya replaced the tube beside the cap and pressed her hands together. She felt the cream escape between her fingers and began to rotate her hands, spreading the suntan lotion evenly. Then she drew herself up on the mattress and began to massage the cream into her naked breasts and shoulders. They were good breasts, there was no escaping the fact. They were firm and ripe, and they stood rather than hung. The aureoles of the nipples were a rich, chocolate brown and the nipples themselves jutted out expectantly like plump, juicy antennae.

Anya saw the line where Black Sea honey gave way to Mediterranean bronze and laid a fresh knout of guilt across her back. Was it so little time ago that she had laid under another sun and thought about another man? She looked down at the soft, glistening flesh undulating beneath her fingers and withdrew her hand abruptly. Her behavior was not *kulturny*. She was not conducting herself like a responsible Soviet citizen with a senior position in one of the most important government departments. But what in her life before the Crimean experience had prepared her for the sybaritic indulgences that the West lavished upon its favored bourgeoisie? Not her one-room flat on the sixth floor of the Sadovaya-Chernogriazskay Ulitz, the women's barracks of the State Security Departments, or her monthly salary of two thousand rubles. Not serving with the rank of Major in the dreaded K.G.B. It must be this sudden role-reversal that had unbalanced her. She must get a grip on herself. Instead of baking her self-indulgent body an unnecessary brown she should be reading an improving work. Something by Engels, for instance. She was shamelessly ill-versed in his writings. Angrily, she pulled her severe one-piece bathing costume over her breasts and slipped the straps across her slim shoulders. She was not to know, that by its very simplicity—and because it was slightly too small for her—the costume made her body seem almost more erotic than it was when naked.

Anya rose to her feet, screwed the top firmly back on the tube of Piz-bruin and folded up the sun mattress. She left the balcony and entered the large cool bedroom, closing the sliding glass door behind her to maintain the air conditioning at its current temperature. Air conditioning! No wonder this suite cost each day nearly as much as her monthly salary. It was shameful. She blushed. Shameful, too, the way she had so easily succumbed to its pleasures. Taking off her costume, she enjoyed the sensation of the cool air against her body and stood on tiptoe to place the sun mattress on top of one of the white louvered cupboards. She would not be using it again. The mirror threw back her reflection, and she felt ashamed of her nakedness, as if she were exposing it to someone else rather than to herself. She must have a shower and put on some clothes. Bond would be back soon, and she did not want the embarrassment of being found undressed. She picked her costume from the double bed and walked toward the bathroom, passing the small bed in which Bond slept. She wondered if he had noticed that every morning she made the bed before any of the maids came in. She had to admit that it was pride that made her do it. She did not want anyone to think that her husband found her sufficiently unattractive to be dismissed from his bed. Not, of course, that she would ever sleep with Bond in a thousand years. Their presence together was for the convenience of the State. He was handsome, yes. Very handsome. One need not be afraid of admitting it. But he was an Engliski Spion who killed swiftly and, apparently, without feeling. Such a man could never touch her—could he? Anya felt a sudden pang of fear.

Mr. and Mrs. Robert Sterling, bearing a striking resemblance to Bond and Anya, had island-hopped from the port of Santa Teresa di Gallura on the northeast coast of Sardinia and were now installed upon the Isla Caprera, one of the scattering of small islands on the fringe of the Bocce di Bonifacio—or, if one was a Corsican looking across the channel toward Sardinia, the Bouches de Bonifacio. Stromberg's Marine Research Laboratory was apparently somewhere on the dark, rocky Corsican coast that rose abruptly from the sea a few miles away. Stromberg owned a large stretch of coastline, and it was reported by the local people that visitors were not welcome. He seldom appeared in public and was taken to and from his island by helicopter.

Anya left the shower and put on a loose-fitting cotton shift that descended to the middle of her well-shaped thighs. To her, the hotel with its crust of tiles, baked white walls and dark vaulted doors and windows looked like a loaf of bread attacked by mice. There was a private beach with a thatched bar surrounded by straw mushrooms—

more mice sheltering underneath?—terraces, shady colonnades, gardens of bougainvillea and broom hibiscus sloping down to the tightly packed shrubs that fringed the sand, and a stone jetty with a small lighthouse at the end of it. And all about, the many-blued sea, changing its colors as it nosed over white sand or nuzzled yellow rocks, smooth as much-handled gold.

A sharp *toot-toot* on the horn of a motorcar drew Anya to the balcony and she looked down to see Bond standing beside a small, bright red, dart-shaped sports car. Her lip began to curl. The car looked brand-new and very expensive.

"I've managed to find us some transport," said Bond cheerfully. "Lotus Esprit—with modifications. Can I interest you in a trial drive, madame? Excellent specifications: five-speed manual gearbox, eight-and-a-half-inch diaphragm-sprung hydraulically operated clutch—"

"I will come down," said Anya, firmly. She arrived within seconds, conscious that the car was already beginning to attract admiring attention from guests and hotel staff. "We do not need such a car. Where does it come from?"

"It's what you might call a company car," said Bond. "It comes with the job."

"Ridiculous!" Anya noticed people turning their heads and lowered her voice. "This car is too—" she sought the right word "—too important. We could have rented an ordinary car."

Bond looked chastened. "I'm sorry you feel like that, darling." He smiled engagingly at an old lady straining to catch word of what she imagined to be the honeymoon couple's first tiff and took Anya's arm. "Let me try to give you some better news. Stromberg has extended an invitation to his establishment. That letter from the President of the Royal Society must have done the trick. I found a note in reception. They're sending a craft to pick us up."

"What did this President say?" asked Anya.

"That I'm a distinguished marine biologist on holiday in the area and would be delighted to pay my respects."

114

Anya's beautiful eyes widened. "But what do you know of marine biology?"

Bond produced his gunmetal case and took out a cigarette. "Very little. I'm hoping that any discussion will revolve about general topics. Specialists very seldom descend to specifics." He smiled drily and glanced at his watch. "You'd better change into something more protective. It could be a little blustery out there."

"It sounds as if there will certainly be bluster." Anya looked appealingly disapproving.

Bond picked up the hand that had stung him. "If you see me getting out of my depth, show him your wedding ring."

An hour later, Bond stood on the deck of a powerful Riva speedboat and watched the jetty receding behind him. Anya, wearing what looked uncommonly like an Hermès scarf around her head, held the rail beside him and gazed imperiously out to sea. They might have been on their way to Cowes Week. Not for the first time, Bond wondered where she got her clothes. The high-waisted cotton jacket, perfectly tailored to reveal her shapely behind. The well-cut trousers with the raised seam. The narrow cork-soled platform sandals. You could comb Moscow from Sokolniki Park to the Romenskoye Shosse and not find clothes like that. The Russians did not usually lavish *haute couture* on home-grown spies. Perhaps she was Nikitin's mistress.

Bond had noticed the undisguisable lust in the man's eyes at Cairo. He shuddered. Fancy having to submit to that blood-steeped butcher. But, somehow, it did not seem possible. Such a girl could not sleep with Nikitin. "Such a girl," he said, but had she not injected poison into him while smiling into his eyes? She was a spy, not the heroine of a romantic novel. Was it this innate wariness that had until now prevented him from closing the distance between them? Partly, yes. Bond knew that M disapproved of what he described as his "womanizing" and thought it second only to drink as a source of potential danger to a spy. He knew, too, that the Head of International Export, although too loyal a servant of any government to ever say so,

115

heartily disapproved of the joint initiative that was being taken and thought it could well do more mischief than good. Bond loved, honored and obeyed M and wished to avoid any indiscretion that would justify his pessimism.

But was it only professional altruism? Was there not also some element of heightened sensual anticipation in holding back from the so-beautiful girl slumbering in the adjacent bed? Was the imagination of the puritan more delicious than the experience of the hedonist?

And what about the fear of rejection? Did this not play its part? Bond sensed that Anya was a warm, passionate girl who wanted to be made love to—but by him? How would their working relationship be affected by an un-reciprocated pass or—he smiled to himself—a reciprocated one? No, on all counts, better to leave it alone for now.

Bond turned his attention to the crew of the Riva. Three hard-faced, blunt-featured, men who looked as if they opened doors with their noses. What were they? Corsicans? Bulgars? They had hardly said a word since Anya and he had come aboard. They were uniformly dressed in blue espadrilles, canvas trousers, and blue T-shirts bearing the fish emblem between the sinister SS motif of the Sigmund Stromberg Steamship line. How insensitive could you get when European memories of the Nazis were so long? It was almost as if the loathed initials were intended to strike fear.

Out of the shelter of the bay, the wind freshened and the sea became choppy. The helmsman gunned the motor and the sharp prow of the Riva rose shark-like as if bent on devouring the gaunt outcrop of land it was bearing down on. Only seabirds could be seen wheeling about the steep cliff faces, and white water showed where grotesquely shaped needles of rock broke the surface. It was a bleak and dismal place to find sandwiched between the holiday-brochure blues of sea and sky. Why should Stromberg favor such a remote spot when the Costa Smeralda contained so much that was available and beautiful?

The wake of the Riva curved and the distant view of Caprera disappeared as the powerful speedboat plowed its white furrow around the headland. No sign of habitation.

Only headlands of rock and the odd bush peering from a fissure. Where could this marine research laboratory be? And then, quite suddenly, they saw it. The Riva nosed hard to starboard and a gap between two wall of rock opened into a natural harbor enclosing a structure that rose fifty feet above the water. At first glance it resembled a drilling rig topped by a glass dome. Huge, stressed-steel columns at all corners, catwalks, spiral staircases, a tubular elevator shaft to the platform of the dome. On the dome were radio aerials and a radar shield and inside it a Bell YUH-IB Compound Research Helicopter.

Bond sucked breath between his teeth. This was something. But a marine research laboratory? It looked more like a military installation. Bond looked at Anya. Her pensive face suggested that she shared his view.

"Jolly impressive, isn't it, darling?"

Anya saw one of the crewmen staring at her intently and switched on a captivating smile. "Yes, but I was not expecting it to be actually in the sea."

"Couldn't ask for a better place for it." Bond's eyes searched the rocky shoreline. There was a ramp with a winch, some oil drums, and three prefabricated huts. Probably where the crewmen lived. He looked back toward the laboratory. There were perhaps a dozen men watching from the gantries, two of them carrying what were soon revealed to be automatic carbines. They looked down, surly and malevolent, as the Riva nosed against a pontoon jetty and one of the crewmen jumped onto it with the painter. Bond gazed down into the viridescent depths. It was strange but there, where the sea whirled over the metal piles and shoals of small fish hung immobile, he could see what looked like the outlines of ballast tanks. What purpose would they serve on this permanent structure?

"*Signore!*" The tone was as peremptory as the outstretched arm gesturing toward the jetty, and the accent was not Italian. It came from farther east, Bond was sure of it.

"Mind how you step, darling. It's very slippery." Bond gave Anya his arm and looked at the thin stains of rust

117

leaking from the bolts above his head. Curious the exposure to the elements in this sheltered little cove with its high cliff walls that shut out the sun even as midday was approaching.

A flight of steps led to the core of the structure, and one of the crewmen pressed a button in the wall. A door slid open, and Bond saw the inside of a small elevator. He was waving Anya into it when one of the other men shook his head. "*Signor* Stromberg wishes to see you alone. The *signorina* will stay with us."

Bond tried to appear unthrown. "I see. Going to give her a conducted tour. Good idea. You've seen enough fish to last you a lifetime, haven't you, darling?"

Was there a slight hint of alarm in her eyes as he stepped into the elevator? He rather hoped so. Certainly, he was feeling tense himself, the pulse quickening, a slight drying in the back of the throat that made him want to swallow. The elevator sank silently and trembled to a halt. A pause, and the door slid back with a soft hiss. Bond stepped forward and paused. After the bright Mediterranean light this was like going into a darkened auditorium. The door slid shut behind him and Bond's eyes tested the gloom. There was no sign of Stromberg. The silence lay thick as the pile on the deep carpets. But though there was silence, there was movement. Brightly colored movement. Both sides of the sixty-foot-long room formed the armored-glass walls of aquariums. Ingeniously designed lighting made the endless streams of fish that glided past seem like some psychedelic back-projection. Living, moving wallpaper. Bond stepped to the nearest wall and found himself face to face with a cherry-pink snapper that was nosing the glass and slowly opening and shutting its mouth as if blowing him kisses. A shoal of angelfish shimmered past. Bond turned around slowly. What a conception. The cost of building the aquariums and assembling the collection must have been astronomical. If this was a front, it was the most expensive front in history.

"Why do we seek to conquer space when seven-tenths of our own universe remains unexplored?"

At first, Bond thought the voice was coming over a

loudspeaker system. It had the same didactic, disembodied quality of a talking guide cassette in a museum. Then he turned and saw the tall, slim figure silhouetted against the moving fish. How he had appeared so silently and suddenly was almost disturbing. Bond felt the small hairs on the back of his neck begin to prickle.

"Mr. Stromberg? How do you do. My name is Sterling. Robert Sterling. It's most awfully kind of you to receive me like this. I do hope I'm not disturbing your routine too much? Couldn't resist making contact when I knew I was going to be in the area." Bond grasped the hand of corpselike coldness that slowly advanced to meet his own and tried to read messages in the extraordinary oval face. Perhaps it was the light, but the features seemed so indistinct that they might have been painted in water colors on an eggshell. Was this whey-faced, insubstantial creature the ruthless founder of the Stromberg empire?

"Quite agree with the point you were making about oceanic exploration." Bond babbled on in his guise of hearty academic. "Still, if the rest of your operation is anything on this scale you seem well prepared to rectify the oversight. Tell me. What prompted you to build your laboratory here?"

Stromberg's eyes bored into him. "You will probably have noticed that the natural harbor in which we are situated is formed by the caldera of a volcano that exploded three thousand years ago—we are in fact on the most northerly sector of the Ligurian Tyrrhenian volcanic arc passing through Vesuvius and Etna. I hope that I will eventually be able to build harbor gates so that the whole area of the caldera can be turned into a fish farm and site for the development of maritime resources."

"Fascinating," said Bond. "I wondered why you chose to cut yourself off from the more obvious pleasures of the Costa Smeralda."

"I invent the obvious, Mr. Sterling." Stromberg's eyes glittered dully. "Only, when I invent it, it is unique. That is why I enjoy a generous measure of commercial success." He suddenly walked to the wall of an aquarium and tapped on the glass. "Tell me. What is the name of this variety?"

119

Bond felt his stomach turn to ice. The sudden change of subject and the aggressive edge to the voice were contemptuously chilling. It was like being interviewed for a job and hearing the interviewer's chair scrape back. He advanced toward the glass feeling as if someone had applied a coating of talcum powder to the roof of his mouth. Stromberg was watching him intently. What the devil could he say? That he had left his spectacles at the hotel and was blind without them? How ridiculously lame it sounded. He peered into the tank. My God! Could it be true? He looked again. What a fantastic coincidence. The chap he had shared a study with at school had kept two of those. He remembered the outlandish Latin name.

"Well?"

"You mean the *Pachypanchax playfairi?*" Bond's voice was casual to the point of ennui. "The Thick Panchax." He tapped the glass as if it was the window of a petshop with a particularly beguiling puppy behind it. "Happy little chap, isn't he?" Bond turned away and walked as swiftly as he dared toward a glass case lit from inside. "What's this?"

"Something that I think you'll find very interesting, Mr. Sterling." There was no warmth in the voice, but the edge of distrustful menace had been blunted. "A plan that I am developing. It's a project very close to my heart."

"You mean, you're developing the plans, not the city?" asked Bond.

"It's not beyond the realm of possibility or necessity that one will lead from the other." Stromberg's small, sphincter mouth had devoured its lips and his face glowed with a strange luminous sheen. Bond was glad to look down into the case. It clearly represented the bed of the ocean and showed glass-domed buildings joined by transparent corridors. Like living in a goldfish bowl, he thought to himself. Models of frogmen on underwater sleds tending shoals of net-bound fish or crops planted in orderly lines along the ocean bed. Bulldozers clearing away outcrops of rock. Most imposing of all, the laboratory standing in the middle of the whole structure. The axle from which the spokes

120

radiated. It must all be feasible. Bond wondered what kind of comment would be appropriate.

"How long do you envisage people staying down there?"

A chilling intensity froze the liquid eyes. "Indefinitely, Mr. Sterling."

There was a challenge in the voice, but before Bond could consider a means of answering it, he was saved by the soft, muted warbling of a concealed telephone.

"Excuse me, Mr. Sterling."

Stromberg crossed to the wall by the elevator and opened a concealed cupboard. The incongruous warbling stopped. Bond turned toward the far aquarium as a huge gray shadow passed across the glass and then swung abruptly away. A shark. And a big one. It must have been fourteen feet, at least. Bond moved forward and his jaw tightened as the sinister flat head planed in toward him. The half-moon mouth seemed to be set in a contemptuous sneer, as if daring him to cross the glass barrier that divided them, and the flick of the turning tail was dismissive.

Bond watched the shark disappear into the cobalt gloom and wondered how far back the aquarium went. There seemed to be some gap in the rocks like the entrance to a tunnel. He was about to turn away when something emerged from the tunnel. A large spider-crab clutching an object in one of its pincers. Bond peered forward. The crab was dragging a human hand, severed at the wrist. The flesh was a hideous, glaucous green, but the long female nails, with one exception, were intact. Bond controlled a desire to retch.

"I am sorry, Mr. Sterling—" Stromberg had materialized behind him like a ghost. Had he too seen the hand? Bond turned away and tried to appear composed before the searching eyes that fed on secrets. "Something has arisen that requires my urgent attention. I hope you will forgive me if I bring our meeting to a close. At least you will have enjoyed a small maritime excursion."

"Oh, much more." Bond could feel his legs carrying him toward the elevator as if operating under their own volition." Just to catch a glimpse of your operation was a privilege."

Stromberg pressed a button and the elevator door slid open. "Goodbye, Mr. Sterling. We never had an opportunity to discuss your activities, but I wish you success with them."

Bond inclined his head deferentially. "What I've seen today encourages me to redouble my efforts. Goodbye, Mr. Stromberg."

The elevator door closed, and for several seconds Stromberg continued to stare at it reflectively. He then crossed to the aquarium where Bond had last been standing and looked downward. His was not a face on which it was easy to read expressions but a faint cloud of preoccupation wrinkled the serene brow. Obediently, the swivelling lenses of the closed-circuit television followed his every move and awaited the inevitable summons. Stromberg was still looking at the floor of the tank when he eventually spoke.

"Send Jaws in. There is more work to be done."

Chapter 15

MOTORCYCLES ARE DANGEROUS

"Comfortable?" asked Bond.

"Physically, yes. Mentally, less so." Anya looked at him challengingly. "It does not seem to be the moment to go riding in fast sports cars."

Bond coaxed the Esprit's stubby gear-stick into first. "Fasten your seat belt. You'll enjoy it more."

"But where are we going?"

"I want to take a closer look at Stromberg's laboratory."

"We could take a boat from the hotel."

"Too risky, I think Stromberg has a number of friends at the hotel. They'd soon be on the radio to him. Has your baggage been searched?"

Anya looked at him sharply. "I thought it was you."

Bond smiled. "Not guilty. I've had everything searched —and by experts. They even checked the heels of my shoes. I found the marks where they'd been prising out the nails."

Bond paused while a small, nut-brown child retrieved her beach ball from beneath the wheels, and slowly took the car down the drive.

Anya settled back against the headrest and stretched out her legs. "So we're going to approach the island from a different direction." Bond raised approving eyes from legs to road. "Exactly." He paused at the entrance to the drive and swung the wheel to the left. The Lotus came around like a whippet with its nose down on a rabbit and the race-proved two-liter 907 engine began to bubble happily as the revs built up. Anya watched the expression of tight-lipped anticipation on Bond's face and smiled to herself. He was like a child with a new toy.

"Do you think they could operate the tracking system from the laboratory?"

Bond frowned. "It's feasible, I suppose. What I don't understand is how they could have sunk the submarines—if that's what happened." He did a racing change and blessed the telescopic shock absorbers as the Esprit ironed out a pothole and swung around a corner as if hooked onto a rail.

Anya shrank back into the bucket seat. "Do you always drive like this?"

Bond darted a glance at her. "No. Sometimes I speed a little." A piece of straight road loomed up and the needle flickered against the hundred mark. "How did your con-ducted tour go?"

"Very slowly. Nobody understood my questions, or at least, they pretended not to. But some of those men were Bulgars, I would swear it. They understand Russian."

"So you saw nothing? No laboratories? No unusual equipment?"

"They showed me a kind of sitting room. That was most untechnical. Very old-fashioned, in fact—except for the model of a tanker. The latest addition to the Stromberg line. It is called the *Lepadus*. It weighs over six hundred thousand tons."

Bond whistled through his teeth. "It must be the biggest in the world."

Anya's chin lifted proudly. "After the *Karl Marx*."

Bond sighed and slipped past a truck while the driver wondered why he had never seen him coming up in the rear-view mirror. "I might have guessed. Maybe it would

124

be a good idea to check out this *Lepadus*. I'll get on to M about it."

Anya leaned across and tapped Bond lightly on the knee. "That will not be necessary, James"—she pronounced it "Shems" which Bond found rather charming—"I have already contacted our information service."

Bond nodded and pursed his lips. It would be foolish to underestimate Major Amasova. She was the ultimate proof that beauty and brains could go together. He glanced in the rear-view mirror and frowned. That was funny—the motorcycle and sidecar that had suddenly appeared behind them. The sea was on one side, a hundred feet below a low stone wall, and there was sheer cliff on the other. The motorcycle must have been in a cut-off. It was almost as if it had been waiting for them. Bond put his foot down, and the Lotus surged forward. Anya caught up with her stomach and followed Bond's checking eyes.

"Do you think we're being followed?"

"Possibly. But they won't be able to live with us in that thing. I'd be more worried if there was anyone in the sidecar." Bond put his foot down and flicked into fourth as the needle hovered around the ninety mark. The mounting excitement of the Grand Prix engine settled into a contented bay. Ahead was a long stretch of straight road with the sea twinkling far below.

"He's dropping back—James! I think he's on fire."

Bond's eyes shot to the mirror. At first glance, it seemed as if Anya was right. Smoke was streaming from behind the sidecar and there was a glimpse of yellow flame. Bond suppressed a smile. Serve the fellow right. It was an impertinence to try to keep up with the Lotus in that thing. Then Bond looked again. The combination was actually breaking up! There was a ferocious wobble and the motorcycle veered off to the left. Bond watched in amazement. The sidecar was still coming on! In a second, the momentum would slacken and the sidecar would crash into the stone wall.

But the momentum did not slacken.

"James! It's coming for us!"

Anya was right. Like a land torpedo, the sidecar was

trailing a growing tail of yellow flame and gaining on them fast. Bond drove the accelerator pedal down until his foot was flattening the carpet pile. The engine roared enthusiastically, and the rev counter climbed toward the six thousand mark. A hundred and twenty, a hundred and twenty-five—racing change into fifth—a hundred and thirty, a hundred and thirty-five. The needle was still climbing but—

"It's gaining on us!"

What the devil was it? Some kind of guided missile programmed to destroy them? Was there no way of shaking it off? Bond searched the road ahead. They were coming up fast behind a furniture van. Bond read the Italian on the back: The Mandami Mattress Company. Well, it was soon going to be sweet dreams—unless—Bond shot toward the van as if intent on ramming it and felt Anya tensing beside him. The wedge nose of the Esprit trembled under the tailboard, and he glanced at the mirror. Death dressed in yellow and orange was streaking toward them. Bond threw the wheel over and heard Anya scream. A trailer truck filled the road. Its headlights swore at him, but Bond's pressure on the accelerator pedal did not slacken. As the wall of metal bore down on them, the Lotus rippled and then hurled itself forward. There was an eldritch wail like an express train passing in the night, and the world disintegrated into a kaleidoscope of smeared vision and ruptured sound. Bond jerked the wheel to the right, and the car skipped into line behind him. Suddenly, the road in front was empty. Thank God! The tension released itself as if through an opened valve. He glanced at the mirror. Behind, it was snowing. The road was obscured by a blizzard of white flakes. Not snowflakes, feathers! The sidecar had detonated on impact with the van and blown God knows how many feather mattresses to kingdom come. In hot pursuit, the motorcyclist, half blinded by feathers, lost control of his machine. The bike twisted like a rubber band and went through the low wall as if it was piecrust. For an instant it seemed to hang in space, then traced a graceful parabola to the ocean. Driver and machine were not separated when they hit the water. Bond's cruel face looked down at the widening, froth-flecked ripples without expression. He shook his head.

"All those feathers, and he still couldn't fly."

The cloud of feathers began to disperse and drift toward the sea, revealing the charred superstructure of the van. Flames licked through the roof and the driver stood beside the still-intact cab of his blazing vehicle and semaphored his feelings to heaven.

Bond watched as a battered Fiat saloon picked its way through the wreckage and waited for the occupants to come stumbling out and join the van driver in a pantomime of Latin gesticulation. But the Fiat did not stop. Clear of the obstruction, it picked up speed and came toward them. Fast. Bond jerked his head around and the 14-inch 7Js blitzed gravel against the perimeter wall. In five seconds the needle had passed fifty and the Lotus was filling its lungs with power. The Fiat hurtled after them, and the chase was on. Bond glanced in the mirror and his jaw tightened. The Fiat was holding on well. Something must have been souped up under that rusty hood. As he looked, a figure leaned out of one of the windows and something glinted. *Crack! Crack!* Two single shots, and then a burst of automatic fire. Bond sawed at the wheel and swung the Lotus from side to side as a bend loomed up. For a fraction of a second, an oncoming car hung before them and Bond saw a close-up of the driver's terrified face. Then they were in a tunnel—so fast that Bond had no time to flick up the headlights. A semicircle of light became huge before them and bullets hurled chunks of rock against the side of the car. Out of the corner of his eye, Bond could see that Anya had her Beretta in her hand. She turned toward the window.

"Don't bother."

"But—"

"I know you're a crack shot." Bond smiled grimly and drifted into a bend. The tail of the Lotus swung out and then snapped back with a seductive wriggle. "I've done some research on you, as well." He glanced at the dashboard. "How far behind are they?"

"Thirty meters."

"It's what my old Scottish nanny used to call 'Bye-bye time'." He pressed a switch. Nothing happened. Cursing, he pressed it again.

Anya said nothing. She merely leaned out of her window and squeezed off two shots. The cracks were barely audible over the roar of the wind and the engine. The Fiat held its course for a few moments and then slewed violently across the road. Its wheels seemed to fold under it and it snapped off a hollow bollard like a rotten tooth and plunged down a steep incline. The gas tank exploded on the first bounce and like a fireball aimed at hell the Fiat plummeted on to the rocks three hundred feet below. There was a second, more violent explosion and a column of black smoke to mark the spot for the fast disappearing Lotus.

Bond avoided Anya's eyes. "Back to the drawing board," he said ruefully. He eased his foot off the accelerator as the road began to snake down towards the sea. He looked down towards the welcoming blue ocean and thought of the human mincemeat frying at its edge. How much luck did he have left?

"Somebody must have called the *polizia*." Anya was looking along the coast to where a helicopter was approaching at speed. Bond frowned. It was too early to be certain, but it looked like a Bell YUH-IB. The model under the glass dome at Stromberg's laboratory. He began to gun the motor.

"It is coming so fast!"

Bond's eyes were worried slits. "It's probably been fitted with auxiliary turbojets. Should be capable of over three hundred miles an hour." Twice as fast as the Lotus. And it was following the line of the road. The next seconds were crucial. If it was the police, it would stop at the burned-out van. Bond swung into a hairpin and the helicopter was blotted from view. Right hand, left hand, foot down. He looked back. Nothing. A feeling of relief swept over him. He must guard against getting jumpy.

Then it was on them, like an angry dragonfly swooping over the lee of the hill. The sudden roar of the props made his nerves scream, and there was the deadly hammer of cannon fire. A line of shells blasted the road in front of him and stitched a seam of dust explosions up the banking. Bond started to drive like a madman. He had to get down to sea level! *Thud! Thud! Thud! Thud!* The chopper was coming in again, opening up at the road behind them and letting its superior speed do the rest. Anya could see the line of shells racing toward them like a shark's fin toward its victim. Then suddenly there was darkness and a receding circle of light. They were in another tunnel. She turned to Bond. "Why don't we stay here?"

The callous eyes stared unflinchingly ahead. "Because we'd be trapped. They'd drop somebody at either end and shoot us to pieces."

Now they were out of the tunnel and sweeping down toward the sea, protected by high banking. Anya could see the water twinkling twenty feet below her. The sky above was empty. Had the helicopter called off the chase? It was probably still climbing over the rock they had just sped through.

Then it was on them again like an avenging blade. The maneuverability of the Bell was extraordinary. It might have been pinned to their tail. The road opened up, and Anya's heart fell. It ran beside the sea, straight and level as a landing strip. There was no escape route. They would have to stop and fight at any cover that presented itself. But Bond did not stop. His foot pressed down and his ruthless jaw set firmer. What was he trying to do? He could not outspeed the helicopter. The road stretched straight for as far as the eye could see. Anya looked back. The helicopter was five feet above the ground and coming up on them as if intending to land on the roof of the car. She could see the pilot and the huge bulk of the man beside him.

Stromberg's killer. His mouth was split into a smile of triumph and his hands were wrapped exultantly about the cannon at if it was a toy that had at last come into its own. He was going to open up at them from point-blank range; the heavy shells would tear the G.F.R.P. bodywork to reinforced-plastic shreds and spew their guts over three hundred meters of tarmac.

"Stop!"

Bond stamped the brake pedal through the floor and left two ribbons of burning rubber spilling out like insulating tape. The Lotus began to spin and the chopper overshot the car and soared like a swingboat in its upward arc. As it banked steeply and returned, Bond conquered the spin and flung the wheel toward the sea. The Esprit shuddered into its new alignment and burst forward onto a small apron of hardtop. Anya glimpsed sea all around her and heard the cannon begin to hammer her death knell. For a moment they were still and then the sinews of Bond's wrist locked and the Lotus flew toward a narrow jetty with two yachts moored against it. She heard the thump of the planks beneath the tires and then they were in mid-air. The golden sun fused with a million malachite motes and then the nose went down and the sea rushed up to claim them. Anya closed her eyes, and braced herself against the impact.

From the helicopter, Jaws watched the Lotus plunge into the sea and felt angry. The man had cheated him even in death. He ordered the pilot to fly over the spot and strafed the sea with cannon shells. But there was no comforting patch of red. Only dark, swirling weed to show where the car was lying. The Bell made another pass and then side-slipped away toward Stromberg's laboratory.

Chapter 16

ESPRIT DE MORT

The Lotus sank like a tidbit dropped into a fish tank. Anya looked at the dark green death closing in about her and tried not to panic. It was fortunate that the car was shaped like a dart, but the safety strap had still bruised her breasts when they hit the water. The car wavered from side to side like a falling leaf and settled in a bank of weed. The tentacles waved menacingly against the windows as if eager to gain entrance and envelop them. Anya fought a desire to scream.

"All right?" Bond's brisk inquiry might have followed the car's lurching over a pothole.

"I am still alive." Anya leaned forward and saw the opaque glass surface of the water twenty feet above her head. A spiral of spent cannon shells dropped to land on the hood. She looked to her right and saw that the bottom of the door was hard against a rock. At least no water seemed to be coming in. What were the rules for escaping from submerged cars? Open windows sufficiently to flood car slowly; when pressures are equal, inside and out, there will be no resistance to doors opening. But on her side there would be resistance. The rock. Bond was looking up toward the surface. "I think he's gone. He must reckon we've had it." He sounded almost cheerful.

"Haven't we?"

"I hope not." Bond stabbed the dashboard and there was a slow whirring sound like a diesel engine starting up. Another switch and the headlights popped out of the hood and reached into the gloom. Bond gritted his teeth and pushed hard down on the gear lever until it almost disappeared into its rubber cowling. Anya watched in amazement. "You cannot drive under the sea!" Bond slid the knob of the gear lever forward, and the Lotus quivered like a hovercraft preparing for flight and then smoothly drew away from the bank of weed. "Not on wheels. Welcome to Wet Nellie. Incidentally, don't let anyone in Q Branch hear you call it that. To them she will always be the QST/A117 Submersible."

Anya looked at Bond, and her eyes narrowed angrily. "All the time you intended to do this, but you would not tell me!"

"I didn't have a lot of chance once our friends came calling. Anyhow, it's all for the best. Once the helicopter reports in, Stromberg won't be expecting visitors." Bond twisted the gear lever knob, and the Lotus veered to port.

"How long can we stay down?" Anya was impressed but she judged it impolitic to show it too readily.

"As long as the fuel holds out, and we've got enough for our purpose. Air is no problem as there's a small regenerative plant." Bond grinned. "All other information is classified."

Anya was irritated by Bond's smile. "I do not think you will find the Soviet Union behind in such developments."

"I'd better keep my eyes open, then." Bond pressed his face against the windshield. "It would be embarrassing if we bumped into one of yours, wouldn't it?"

Anya made a face and settled back in her seat. She was getting used to Bond now. Perhaps he was not so bad as she had once thought. It would be difficult to survive what they had just gone through together without feeling something, even if it was only a sense of shared experience. She looked at the ruthless face out of the corner of her eye and detected a slight complacent smile indenting one corner of his mouth. It was almost as if he was aware of what she was thinking. The thought made her pull her eyes severely to the front. Her attitude to the English spy must remain inflexible. That was the only way she could perform her duty to the State. Whatever she did, she must not fall in love with him.

Bond steered from a compass set in the dashboard and after ten minutes brought the Lotus up to a point just below the surface. He pressed a button on the dashboard, and a periscope tube rose from its housing where the hood joined the windshield. As this broke the surface, Bond slid open a panel set in the broad center band of the driving wheel and a small television screen was revealed. Bond twisted the knob on the dashboard and the seascape on the screen started to turn through three hundred and sixty degrees.

"Excellent!" Bond's remark heralded the appearance of Stromberg's cliffs, gaunt and sharp as a blackened tooth. "I'll take her in and we'll nose our way around to the caldera."

It was noticeable that there was more current running now, and the water became turbulent and cloudy. Visibility was bad, and the headlights bounced back as if playing on thick fog. A column of rock reared up dangerously close and the Lotus bobbed past, nearly scraping its side. Shingle rattled against the bottom of the car like shaken dice. There was obviously a treacherous undercurrent. Bond thought of the jagged fingers of rock seen from the Riva and headed out to sea. Better to back off and take another look through the periscope. This he did and came in straight toward the narrow opening between the rocks at a depth of two fathoms. It was noticeable that the moment the opening was breached, the sea bed disappeared beneath them. The explosion, millenia before, had clearly blasted a huge hole in the earth into which the sea had rushed.

What was less obvious was the position of the two electric eyes staring at each other from opposite sides of the channel.

Once the contact between them was broken a message was immediately flashed to the operations room of Stromberg's laboratory.

Bond was thinking about the depth of the caldera. Why build in its middle when an easier foundation could be found nearer the shore or actually on it? Perhaps the caldera had been formed by the explosion of two adjacent volcanoes and there was an underwater ridge between them. Bond cut back power and went down to four fathoms. It would be interesting to see what the laboratory was built on.

"I'm going in. Keep your eyes peeled."

Anya nodded and hunched forward. Bond was reminded of her posture when the microfilm had been expected at Cairo. Keen. That was the word for it.

The water inside the natural harbor was calm, but the visibility was still bad, probably as a result of the sea's reaction with the sulphurous compounds on the inside of the caldera. Bond's eyes probed the gloom and he became prey to a strange sense of apprehension. He could almost feel Stromberg watching him from the perimeter of his vision. The all-seeing watery gaze filtering toward him. So strong was the image that when Bond saw the inverted dome he shrank back in his seat. For a moment it seemed like a gargantuan replica of Stromberg's head lolling backwards in the water.

"James!" Bond looked down to see Anya's hand gripping his wrist. "That is it. It is not a permanent structure. It floats!"

Anya was right. He might have been looking up at the hull of a ship. There was no foundation. No sign of mooring. The heavy base of the structure hung in the water like the bottom of a saucepan. But why? Was it so that the laboratory could be towed to other locations? This seemed the only feasible explanation—and not a bad idea, either. Stromberg could play with his expensive toy anywhere in the world. Its range was infinite.

Bond caught a movement out of the corner of his eye. A depth charge! No sooner had he sent the Lotus plunging toward the murky depths then there was a violent explosion and his head crashed against the side of the car. He could feel the blood running down from his temple and the dreadful, vibrating pain burrowing into his eardrums like a drill. The shock waves slapped the Esprit sideways and water started to splutter through leaks in its buckled frame. A dead sea bream cannoned off the windshield like a spattered fly. A second explosion rippled them farther into the depths and Bond desperately tried to feel some response from the controls. He looked at the compass. The needle spun aimlessly. He had to find his way out by instinct. One thing he knew for certain. He dared not go any deeper, or the pressure would destroy them. There was still no sign of the bottom. Bond twisted the directional control and felt his shirt sticking to his body. If the steering had been hit, they were doomed.

Boom! Another depth charge. A moray eel snapped past in its death agonies, precursor of a twitching pall of dying fish. Bond tried to keep calm and twisted the steering knob like a burglar feeling for the combination of a safe. Beside him, Anya tore a strip of material from her shirt and forced it into one of the cracks through which water was seeping. At last! Bond felt the Lotus turning in the direction he wanted it to and gingerly increased speed. To crash into the side of the caldera would be to commit suicide. With every second that passed he waited for sight or sound of the next depth charge that must surely destroy them, but there was nothing. Visibility was still down to half a dozen yards.

"James!" Bond turned his head and had just enough time to see the frogman aligning what looked like a slim torpedo mounted on the wall of the caldera. Then he put the Lotus into a bank as the weapon was fired. Like an arrow the torpedo sped toward them, and for a second Bond thought that it was equipped with some magnetic device that would home in on them. Then it streaked underneath the front of the tilting car and exploded with a flash against the side of the caldera. Once again, the Lotus was shrugged aside but this time the light of the explosion

135

gave Bond a split-second glimpse of what lay in front. Fifty feet ahead was the harbor opening.

"James! There are others behind!"

Anya was right. Three frogmen pushing rocket-launchers were closing the distance toward them. At any second, they would fire. Bond jabbed a finger at the dashboard, and a cloud of black ink wiped out Anya's view of the pursuers. "Also known as Billy the Squid," said Bond. His eyes probed the dim light ahead. "Ah! I see the car-park attendants are gathering to collect their dues." Three frogmen carrying what looked like crossbows were positioned in front of a chain fence that now covered the opening they had entered by.

Anya felt powerless and envious of the grim confidence in Bond's voice. All three frogmen were levelling their weapons as he leaned forward and pulled a lever beneath the dashboard. There was a sigh and a louvered metal screen rose up to cover the windshield like a venetian blind. A spurt of bubbles showed that one of the frogmen had fired and his bolt thumped into the louvers. There was a sharp crack and a seam of water ran down the inside of the windshield.

Bond felt icy fingers of fear tightening around his stomach. A shot from the side would finish them. He had not expected the louvers to be so easily breached. The second man fired his bolt and missed. Bond pulled another lever and two small hatches beside the front indicator lights slid open. Behind them were the recessed barrels of two 2.3 rocket-launchers. Bond levelled at the third man and pulled the triggering mechanism. There was an instant recoil, and for a second Bond was not certain whether they had been hit. The car shook, and more water came in through the cracked windshield.

Then they saw the man going down, trailing blood and entrails. Anya sucked in her breath in horror. Bond fired the second rocket and tore a hole in the steel netting. But was it wide enough? There was only one way to find out, made doubly dangerous by the fact that Bond dared not accelerate for fear of upsetting the delicate balance of the damaged steering. Fighting to keep the car steady, he headed for the narrow opening. Another frogman appeared directly in his path, but there was no deviation. As the man held out his gun to shoot, Bond drove the wedge nose of the Lotus into him and propelled him backwards draped over the hood of the car like a rag doll. His face was so close that Bond could see the terror in the man's eyes. Then he was pushed back into the wire so that the severed strands ripped the wetsuit from his back like sharpened claws and once again the water turned red with blood. The grip of the wire tightened around the Lotus as it thrust deeper into the breach, and Bond could see that the strands were as thick as a man's thumb.

Dry-mouthed, he opened the throttle as far as he dared and listened to the nerve-shredding screech of the wire as it slowly scraped along the roof of the car. Beside him, Anya sat tight-lipped, waiting, as he was, for the missile that would come gliding out of the inky black darkness behind them. Inch by painstaking inch the Esprit moved forward, seeming to carry the whole fence with it, and then—*Boom!* Another depth charge. Another series of surging shock waves. Bond closed his eyes and clapped his hands to his ears to deaden the pain. Then he felt the nose of the Lotus dropping. They were no longer trapped in the wire! The explosion had pushed them through. Bond looked back and saw the fence shimmering into place, the ruptured wires reaching out like hungry tentacles robbed of their prey. Dropping down to the floor of the ocean, he took the Lotus swiftly toward the cover of the nearest rocks.

Chapter 17

RED ROSES FOR A RED LADY

The fortuitous, amazing and unprecedented escape of the newlyweds soon became by far the most compelling topic of conversation at the Hotel Carla di Volpe. Everybody agreed that had Mr. and Mrs. Sterling perished, it would have quite ruined their holiday—they were of course referring to their own holidays—and it just showed how careful you had to be if you were fortunate enough to be the owner of what was clearly a very expensive sports car. Money could not buy good health, and it was worth almost any price to be reminded of this fact. The whole incident, regrettable as it was would obviously teach Mr. and Mrs. Sterling a very valuable lesson and one that would stand them in good stead in the years to come. They would become more sober, diligent, and unobtrusive, and might, with any luck, even become less self-confident, physically attractive, and transparently rich. Still, it was pointless discussing luck in the presence of such people because they obviously already enjoyed a superabundance of it. To plunge into the sea in a motorcar and survive was very lucky. To plunge into the sea at a marina and be able to winch your car ashore so that it was still drivable required a word stronger than any compounded with luck and not yet found in English, French, German, or Italian dictionaries.

Still, perhaps the handsome cruel-faced man with the arrogant manner did feel a pang of guilt for his behavior and his good fortune, because the extravagantly large bunch of red roses arriving in the chauffeur-driven car were apparently for his wife and must have been ordered at his behest. It was only a gesture—and one that he could easily afford—but it said something on his behalf.

When they limped back to the hotel, Bond had thrown out the first story that came into his head to explain the condition of the Lotus and steered Anya up to the suite. He closed the door behind them and looked at her—bruised, bedraggled, and utterly and totally beautiful. She had thrown herself into his arms and clung to him with her arms around his neck. "Oh, James! We are still alive, alive! All the time we sit in that car I think that I am never going to be able to tell you." Her mouth came up eagerly, and he kissed it hard and long, feeling the beautiful strong curve of her body thrusting against his. She was shameless, uncontrolled, spontaneous.

"Dammit, woman! I think I'm falling in love with you." He wanted to say it first.

"Good, good!" She kissed him again, standing on tiptoe. "I cannot believe that we are still alive. I know that it is ridiculous to talk of fate—but, oh, dear James"—again, that haunting 'Shems'—"we must be special, you and I."

Bond looked down into the beautiful, proud face glowing with love and intensity and felt tears prick his eyes. She was so much his woman, so much like another he had loved. "I think, when we are in the car, that if ever again we have the chance to make love, we must take it. I would hate to die without having your body inside mine."

They kissed again, and this time it was like some kind of sacrament. The act went beyond the physical manifestation of their two bodies melding together. Bond felt himself closer to this woman than if they had been making love. He kissed her deeply and then drew away, waiting to hear a loud click at the back of his brain and discover that he had been dreaming. Nothing happened. The brave blue eyes still stared quizzically into his. The proud nose tilted up a millimeter. The soft, lustrous mouth said "I desire you" without parting its lips.

"I hope you realize that you were appearing flamboyantly provocative in the foyer? Old men were falling off the bar stools like ninepins." Bond looked down at the slim breasts poking through the remnants of Anya's shirt.

Anya took his hand and pressed it against her breast. "Do not change the subject. I want to make love to you. Have I not made myself clear? I am not interested in the old men." She tightened her grip around his neck. "Now kiss me and take me on the bed—the big bed."

In the circumstances, thought Bond, there is nothing in the world I would rather do. He had an animal longing to make love to this girl. To join her in celebrating that they were still alive.

And then there was a discreet tap on the door. Anya slid her arms from around his neck, and her lower lip pouted petulantly. She looked quickly toward the door and then back to Bond. He could sense what was going through her mind and shook his head gently. "We'd better answer it. That may be duty calling."

Anya rose up to kiss him swiftly on the lips. "Yes my dear. We can wait a little longer. We have all the time in the world."

Her last words hit Bond like a blow across the face. That was what he had said to Tracy just before she was murdered. The words were heavy with premonitions of disaster and death.

"No!" Anya paused, surprised, on her way to the door. Bond fought to appear calm. The spell was broken, but perhaps only for him. He slipped the Walther PPK into his left hand. "You can't be too careful. Stromberg may be returning our call." He opened the door, keeping the gun behind it, and stared into a large bunch of red roses. Behind the roses and practically obscured by them was one of the bellboys, whom Bond recognized.

"Roses for the Signora Sterling."

"Thank you." Bond parted with a note and bore the roses into the room. They looked normal enough.

Anya looked at him questioningly. "James?"

"I'm not responsible, I'm afraid. They probably come from the management—delighted to find that we're still around to pay the bill."

"You are a cynic—and you look silly standing there with those roses. Give them to me and find a vase." She pronounced it "vaize," like an American.

Bond handed over the roses but stood his ground. "I want to find out who they're from. I've hardly laid lips on you, and I have a rival already. It's very disconcerting."

Anya crossed her arms across the roses and peeped around them coquettishly. "Please, James. There is a vase in the bathroom, I think. I will tell you about my lover when you come back."

"It had better be good." Bond turned on his heel. "I'm a Scorpio and we're very passionate and possessive." Behind the banter he was sad. Something had changed, but he wasn't quite certain what.

Anya waited until Bond had left the room and quickly took a slim, square powder compact from her bag. She pressed it open and then pressed another catch that released the mirror. Turning to the roses, she removed the white envelope tucked inside the cellophane and tore it open. She ignored the card it contained but carefully detached the serrated portion of thin lining paper that backed the face of the envelope. This fitted exactly into the space behind the compact mirror. Anya positioned the paper and snapped the mirror into place. In small but legible type a message was now revealed. She began to read as Bond came into the room.

"I hope this is going to be all right. It looks more like a samovar than a vase. That's not going to offend your principles, is it?" Anya looked up at the vase in Bond's hands as if momentarily wondering what he was doing with it.

"No. It will do very well." She paused. "James, I have had an answer to my request for information on the

141

Lepadus. It is very interesting." Her tone was businesslike. She was once more the prisoner of her profession.

Bond put the vase down and smiled. "Red roses. I should have guessed."

Anya took his hand and squeezed it. "James. I do not have to say anything, do I?" She gestured with the compact." This is why we are here. This is the most important thing. We can wait."

Bond kept his thoughts to himself. "What does the message say?"

Anya released his hand and turned away. "The *Lepadus* was launched eighteen months ago at St. Nazaire and delivered four months later. Since that time there is no record of her having made a commercial voyage."

Bond frowned. "She couldn't have been undergoing trials all that time. Perhaps there was some mechanical problem. She might have run aground or been in a collision."

Anya shook her head. "If there was an accident, then all the repairs were done at sea. There are only fourteen harbors in the world capable of receiving a tanker the size of the *Lepadus*, and she has put into none of them."

Bond digested the information. To build a tanker the size of the *Lepadus* must have cost a fortune—many fortunes. Not to put it to work seemed an act of insanity. Unless . . . was it possible that the cost of the *Lepadus* was going to be recouped in other ways than by carrying oil?

"Do you have any idea where she was when the *Potemkin* disappeared?"

Anya nodded slowly. "The same thought occurred to me. Both vessels were in the North Atlantic. The *Lepadus* was one of the ships contacted in case she had picked up any radio messages or seen wreckage."

Bond's eyes narrowed. Anya was right. It was very interesting. Very suspicious, too. A huge, slow-moving *VLCC* tanker might be just the right cover. Nobody would expect it to have the capability to track and destroy a nuclear submarine. Yet it could stay at sea for long periods without exciting any interest, and its enormous bulk could conceal a multitude of technical equipment and armaments.

"When you saw the model of the tanker at Stromberg's laboratory, was there anything unusual about it?"

Anya paused reflectively before replying. "I don't know how important it is, but there was something strange about the bow. Most big tankers have a bulbous bow—you know, pinched and concave to prevent pitching and maintain speed when in ballast." Anya read Bond's quick nod and smiled apologetically. "But I forget. You know this. You were a commander in the navy."

"That's right," said Bond. "In what way was the *Lepadus* different?"

"The bow was straight." Anya shrugged. "It is probably not a thing of great importance. Designs change all the time. Perhaps they have decided that this shape is better for such a huge tanker."

"Perhaps." Bond looked out across the balcony and toward a distant light which was probably a steamer beating its way toward Bonifacio. "But I think we'd better take a closer look, don't you? Maybe this time I can make the necessary arrangements." He reached across and traced a circle on Anya's wrist. "And then we can have dinner. I've been making my own modest researches and they suggest that the *salsiccia seccata* followed by *agnello allo spiedo* are all that's needed to put new heart into us— washed down by a couple of bottles of *Cannonau di Sorso*, of course."

"Of course." Anya snapped her compact shut and looked up into the mysterious dark eyes now lit with a thin light of loving mockery. She wanted him to kiss her. Very hard and very long. But he did not sweep down toward her imploring mouth. Instead, he flicked his finger across the wine-red roses and tossed the card that had arrived with them into her lap. "What does it say? With love from the K.G.B.?"

She looked down because she did not want him to see the desire raging in her eyes. The thin, precise writing on the card was familiar. It emanated from the rough, sandpaper hand of Comrade General Nikitin. She had seen it many times, asking for information concerning officers who were about to be "evaluated."

"Well?" said Bond. "Who is my rival?"

Anya finished reading the card and crumpled it into a small ball. Her face hardened as if she had been forced to withstand a sudden spasm of pain. "Someone you will never see."

Bond nodded and felt the temperature in the room drop. He gestured toward the roses. "I'll leave you to handle those. Flower arrangement has never been my strong suit."

Anya did not look at him, and her grip tightened around the ball of paper in her hand. Would Bond ever realize that the message it contained had been his death warrant? "Anya. Beware! We have just learned that Bond was responsible for the murder of Agent Borzov. Will expect you to take all measures necessary to defend yourself. N."

Chapter 18

DROPPING IN ON THE NAVY

"That's her down there, sir."

The pilot of the British Navy helicopter steadied his hand on the stick and nodded to port. There was an edge of satisfaction in his voice, but whether it stemmed from having made his rendezvous or from having nearly completed his tour of duty it was impossible to say. Certainly, the weather was turning nasty and the U.S.S. *Wayne* would not have been able to stay on the surface much longer. Bond twisted in his seat and looked down at the long gray cigar with the distinctive diving planes jutting out on either side of the twenty-foot sail. An angry, swirling sea was breaking over the hull and beating against the underside of the planes. So this was what a nuclear submarine looked like. Three hundred feet of death capable of turning Great Britain into a large-scale replica of Stromberg's caldera.

"Nice of them to wait up for us."

If the pilot found anything amusing in Bond's remark he was discreet enough to keep it to himself. "They're signalling for us to come in. You'd better get fastened up, sir. You and—er—the Major."

Bond looked into Anya's impassive face and wondered whether there was any other woman in the world who could look appealing in combat coveralls and a helmet. She looked like a Valkyrie, although this was not perhaps an altogether happy comparison. The Valkyrie, he seemed to remember, were given the job of selecting those who were to be slain in battle. Anya's attitude of late had suggested that he would be a prime candidate for the first axe blow. He tried to catch her eye, but she moved toward the back of the cabin and the winching equipment. What the devil had been in that note to make her suddenly change into a block of ice? She had hardly spoken a word to him since she had read and destroyed it.

"I'll be going down to thirty feet, sir."

Bond thanked the pilot and watched the ratings checking his harness and attaching the strop to the winching line. "If you sit down on the floor and put your arms around each other, we'll winch you down together, sir."

The beginnings of a smile exercised Bond's features. Poor Anya. It must be like finding yourself opposite the most undesirable man in the room during a Paul Jones. Still, she deserved the experience. It might be a woman's prerogative to change her mind, but the speed with which Anya had made the change was an abuse of the privilege. Bond sank onto his side and extended his arms upward. Half a dozen witticisms sprang to his lips, but he suppressed them all. There was no need to goad Major Amasova. If he knew anything about women—and Russian women in particular—she would soon explode into a revelation of her natural feelings. Bond hoped that it would not be when she had a gun in her hand.

The hatch cover sprang back and the sound of angry seas drowned the steady thwack-thwack of the rotor blades. A cold wind filled the cabin and Bond watched the pilot's neck muscles tighten as he juggled the controls to hold the chopper steady.

"As soon as you like!"

Anya had laid her body a yard from his, but at the pilot's words she turned her head aside and wriggled her way

146

forward into his arms. One of the men took up the slack on the winch.

"Hang your feet over the edge and I'll give you a push."

Bond did as he was told and felt the spray against the side of his boots. Below, he could hear the sea lashing the hull of the *Wayne*. Anya's head was against his and the smell of her scent found its way to his nostrils. That was the only proof that this was the same girl who had so wantonly and passionately thrust her mouth and body against his, less than two days before. The same girl who had shown him a glimpse of something that he had thought he would never know again. Damn you! he thought as she clung to him without passion or feeling. What the hell are you playing at?

Strong hands pushed him in the middle of the back, and he was dangling in space with Anya in his arms and the harness digging in beneath his armpits. Wind and spray scourged them, and the gray wasteland of white-ribbed ocean disdained all order as it poured over the bows of the submarine. Seen from above, it seemed as if they were dropping into a maelstrom.

"Okay, I got 'em." Bond was glad to hear the American voice sounding so confident. An earthing pole steadied the wire above his head and his feet touched metal as a wave broke over the bridge. Seen from the sail, the sea was a procession of angry white-topped mountains, whipped by a near gale-force wind. An enlisted man moved in and swiftly disconnected the strops. The winching line swung free and immediately began to snake back toward the helicopter. Bond waved and saw a hand return his salute as the hatch door closed and the machine lifted off and tilted away to starboard. Soon it would be back at its carrier home, the pilot and his crew quaffing hot coffee and munching their way through plates of ham and eggs. Bond thought of the dangerous mission that lay ahead and tried not to feel envious. It was not easy. Beside him, Anya looked about her with cold, appraising interest. Her jaw was set, and there was a ruthless, determined glint in her eyes. For the first time since they had left Sardinia, Bond was glad that she was with him. If her presence served no other purpose, it would keep him on his toes.

Bond liked Commander Carter the moment he set eyes on him. He was tall and rangy, almost gangling, in the style of Gary Cooper, and he seemed too big for his small cabin. He had wrinkles around sailor's eyes, but the wrinkles could have come as much from laughter as from staring into bad weather. His hair was a brush of tawny gold and he had a long bony nose forming the mast to a wide thin-lipped mouth. He was the kind of man that women would have found attractive without being able to name one feature that could honestly have been termed handsome. His handshake was firm and dry, and the hand reached out the moment Bond crossed the threshold of the cabin. "Welcome aboard, Commander. And you, Major. It's a—"

Bond watched the eyes narrow in puzzlement as they made contact with Anya. She nodded briskly and removed her helmet to shake out her hair.

"I'm sorry," said Carter. "I wasn't expecting a woman."

"I have the rank of a Major in the Russian Army," said Anya, coldly. "Please treat me accordingly. My sex is immaterial."

For a moment it looked as if Carter was going to disagree. Then he nodded. "Just as you say, Major. Anyway, you're both here, that's the main thing. I was getting worried about you. It's going to be nasty up there for a while."

"We've been fighting to keep on schedule since we left Sardinia," said Bond. "How long do you think it's going to take us to make contact with the *Lepadus?*"

Carter pulled down a chart of the North Atlantic. "If she's where we think she is, and we can maintain a speed in advance of twenty-five knots, we should be in range within ten hours."

Bond smiled to himself. Carter was certainly understating the top speed of his Los Angeles-class submarine. He wondered if it was only for Anya's benefit. "And then we order her to heave to."

Anya's precise voice chipped in. "Under what pretext?"

148

"Leaking oil," said Carter. "The U.S. government is becoming increasingly alarmed by the number of accidents involving tankers and the long-term, wide-scale damage caused by oil pollution. The risks involving a tanker the size of the *Lepadus* are fantastic. Ten million gallons of crude oil have been spilled into U.S. coastal waters this year; the *Torrey Canyon* disaster in the English Channel resulted in thirty million gallons of oil being leaked. Do you know how much oil a tanker the size of the *Lepadus* can carry? Over half a million *tons*."

"I think you're building up to a persuasive argument," said Bond.

Carter looked serious. "I have authority from the U.S. government to stop and examine any vessel which we believe may constitute an environmental or other threat if it enters American coastal waters."

Anya appeared unmoved. "What happens if the *Lepadus* refuses to heave to?"

Carter started to roll up the chart. "I don't think that situation will arise, Major. We are equipped with conventional armament. When the *Wayne* surfaces and they see who we are, I don't believe they're going to give us any trouble."

Anya shrugged, unimpressed. Bond felt his own tremors of unease. "I have a certain sympathy with Major Amasova's wariness," he said. "We have had some contact with this man Stromberg, and he is ruthless and resourceful. I don't believe he'll give up without a fight."

"Then he can have a fight." Carter's jaw set. "My orders are quite explicit. I am going to put a boarding party on that tanker—by force, if necessary. You haven't seen the men I've assembled for this detail, Commander. They are extremely capable."

"I'm certain they are," said Bond. "I'm not trying to criticize the U.S. Navy. I'm just saying that we are up against a formidable adversary."

Carter looked at Bond levelly. "I'll bear that in mind, Commander." He turned toward Anya and his manner relaxed. "Now, I'm certain you'd probably like a shower, Major. You can use the one in my cabin if you like."

Anya's nostrils flared. "It is not necessary to show me special favors, Captain Carter."

Carter smiled wrily. "All the same, I think it might be better if I did." He turned to Bond. "I'll have you shown to your quarters. I think you'll find that you're sharing with the Major, but I guess she takes that all in the line of duty?"

"Absolutely," said Bond.

Bond soon found that if you were a crew member of a U.S. submarine there was no danger of starving to death. The food was excellent and the cheerful atmosphere of informal efficiency that pervaded the ship was endearingly American. Not for the first time, Bond thought that Britain was lucky to possess such allies. He was introduced to the boarding party that had been selected for him and agreed with Carter's assessment. They did look "extremely capable." Their leader, particularly, Petty Officer "Chuck" Coyle. A face misassembled from chunks of weatherbeaten granite, a build like Mount Rainier and a voice like a foghorn with laryngitis. "What flag does this tub carry, chief?" he had asked.

"Liberia."

"Great! We'll be the first guys to get a combat ribbon for attacking Liberia."

Four hours after the interchange, Bond was stirred from uneasy half-sleep. "I think we're there, sir. Assemble aft." He snapped his eyes open and rolled sideways to check the Walther PPK. In the bunk below him, Anya was performing a similar chore with her Beretta. He watched her purposefully slotting home the bullets. "Have you engraved my name on one of them, or are you leaving it to chance?"

Anya looked up at him, and at last there was emotion written on her face. "Sergei Borzov. Does that name mean anything to you?" Bond shook his head. "You murdered him!"

Bond sighed. "I have a double-O prefix. That means—"

"—you are licensed to kill!" Anya's eyes blazed. "I did not hold a licence, but I loved that man!"

"I'm sorry." Bond was serious. "I don't wish to trivialize, but I don't know who you're talking about."

150

"Not long ago, were you not in the French Alps?"

"Oh, yes." There was a hint of relief in Bond's voice. He understood now and felt no guilt. "That man was sent to kill me. It was either him or me. We were both doing a job. There was no premeditation. If he belonged to you . . ."— Bond's voice tapered away—". . . then I am sorry. It was his great misfortune."

Anya's eyes continued to stare up at him, remorseless, unforgiving. She said nothing, but her eyes spoke hate.

Bond felt it necessary to continue. "Anya, we are both in the same business. We are spies. It is a dirty business. We try to believe that the ends justify the means, but we are never sure. We kill, and we hope that others will live. I bear no resentment to this man Borzov."

Anya's lips split into a bitter smile. "Because you are alive!"

"Because I was lucky!" Bond spat the words. "When it is kill or be killed, I kill! So do you. That is the rule of the game." He swung from the bunk and landed silently like a big cat.

Anya glared at him, eyes blazing. When she spoke, the words came with slow, branding menace. "I know the rules of the game I play. When this mission is over, Sergei will be avenged and you will be dead!" She slammed the loaded clip into the butt of the Beretta.

Bond looked down into the beautiful, brave face with the hair disarranged by an attempt at sleep. The determined jaw and the proud, sculpted cheekbones glowered with loathing and defiance. Everything about the face he admired and coveted.

"He must have been quite a man," he said and turned on his heel.

Outside, the submarine hummed with an air of mounting tension that brought back memories of previous missions. Bond zipped up his combat tunic and made his way past the crew's quarters to a narrow companionway leading up to the control room. An enlisted man moved past him, infiltrating his body into the scant space available like a wraith. Like everybody on board, he had adjusted to the demands of operating in a confined area. Bond felt almost clumsy by comparison.

The inside of the control room was like an amalgam of the cockpits of several jumbo jets. Banks of dials, screens, switches, flashing lights, tubes, piping, and multicolored wires. There was a suppressed babble of procedural sound and two rows of sweating, shirt-sleeved men in headphones looking like operators in a telephone exchange. The atmosphere was warm, bordering on hot.

In the middle of it all stood Carter, shoulders slightly stooped. He nodded as Bond approached. "We got her." He turned to the man standing beside him. "Stand by second observation on the target. Up scope."

With a pneumatic hiss, the periscope rose from the well and the periscope assistant snapped down the handles. Carter dropped to his knees on the deck, seized the handles and pressed his eyes to the eyepiece. He rose to his feet with the ascending periscope. "Take a look, Commander."

Bond felt a sense of exhilaration as he stepped forward and took the shiny handles in his hands. The hunter with the target in his sights. And what a target! It was difficult to get an exact idea but she must be more than a quarter of a mile in length. The bridge structure rose from the stern like a small castle, and the bulwarks were cliff-top high above sea level.

Carter heard Bond's sharp intake of breath. "Yep. That's one of your eighty-tennis-court jobs. You know, Jack Nicklaus needs his best drive and a chip shot to play from one end to the other. Do you notice how low she is in the water?"

Bond nodded. "What's that? Ballast?"

"I guess so. If she's not carrying much oil, it must be."

Bond looked up to find Anya standing beside him. He relinquished the periscope and she nodded curtly. It was noticeable that few crew members were so engrossed in their tasks that they could not spare a few seconds to examine Anya's bulky combat uniform for the more obvious signs of the exceptionally desirable female body it contained.

Anya straightened up and brushed hair from her fore-head. "I see that there is a helicopter on the helideck."

Bond turned to Carter. "I can't be certain from this distance but I think it's a Bell YUH-1B. Our friend Strom-berg has a souped-up version of that model. We've bumped into it before."

"So he could be on board? Interesting." A glint came into Carter's eye and his shoulders snapped back. "Okay. Let's take a closer look." He stepped to the periscope and began to snap out orders. "Target bearing . . . Mark! Range . . . Mark! Down scope."

Bond looked toward Anya, but she avoided his eyes. Damn woman! Did she really mean what she had said? Was she going to pump a bullet into his back when it was all over? He wished he could take her in his arms and shake some rough sense into her. In the background, the arcane liturgy of the control room urged the *Wayne* toward its target.

"One division in high power."

"Range six thousand two hundred yards."

"Angle on the bow, starboard sixty."

"Control—torpedo room. Boarding party ready, sir."

The mention of "boarding party" jarred Bond to his senses. Major Anya Amasova could take her beautiful body to hell. He had more important fish to fry. He turned his back on her and prepared to move amidships.

"Best solution for target is one two zero, speed three knots."

"Officer of the deck, come right north and tell man-euvering to make turns for eleven knots."

"Officer of the deck, aye, aye, sir. Right, twenty degrees rudder. Maneuvering—control. Turns for eleven knots."

"Right, twenty degrees rudder, aye . . . Sir, my rudder is right twenty."

"Steady on course, north."

Bond had taken one step toward the torpedo room when the submarine gave a violent lurch and he was hurled side-ways against a bank of instruments. The lights flickered and for a second he thought that they had rammed some underwater obstacle. Men were thrown backwards into

153

untidy heaps on the floor, and Anya was catapulted into his arms. The smooth, orderly build-up of voices performing their preordained tasks gave way to a disjointed babble as the P.A. system exploded into staccato life. "Control—sonar. Total power supplies failure on all sets." "Control—maneuvering . . . We're losing electrical frequency. I'll have to break down the system."

The lights flickered again and a rising high-pitched whine made Bond grit his teeth. The hull of the submarine was vibrating as if an electric drill was playing against it. It was like being inside a tooth while it was being drilled.

"What in God's name is happening?" Carter's face was deathly white.

Another voice came over the P.A. system. "Reactor scram! Reactor scram! We've lost all electrical supplies."

Another shudder raked the ship and the ear-splitting whine sang through the metal. The lights flickered, dimmed, and then went out like a dying candle. At the same instant as the vibration began to die away there was the sound of the ventilation fans slowly running down and stopping. After that, an eerie, nerve-racking silence. Bond could see the luminous dial of Carter's watch and almost hear the man thinking. A pencil rolled across the deck.

Then Carter spoke with firm authority. "Surface! Blow for'd! Blow aft! Full ahead, full rise on both planes. Up scope."

The noise of compressed air rushing into the ballast tanks was deafening, and Anya dug her nails into Bond's combat suit. The submarine shuddered and rose steeply through the water. Anya, realizing that it was not going to break up, released her hold on Bond. Carter clapped his eyes to the periscope and rose with it. The tension in the control room was painful. Men were counting their life expectancy in seconds. They waited in darkness like sinners at the gates of hell. Carter's outline was just recognizable as he swung the periscope through one hundred and eighty degrees. Then there was a gasp. An unbelieving gasp.

"My God! It's not possible!"

Chapter 19

THE TRAP CLOSES

A giant shock wave shook the *Wayne* like a cuff from a huge hand, and Bond was hurled forward into the darkness. He cannoned into one of the crew and sprawled half-stunned across the deck. Around him, men groaned, cursed, and struggled to gain some response from their lifeless equipment. At any second, Bond expected the hull to split and the water to come rushing in. It was the darkness that made it unbearable. They were like cats doomed to drown in a sack. Bond scrambled to his knees and found Carter as a second but lesser shock wave ran through the submarine. There was a distant booming noise from the stern as if someone was hitting the hull with a sledgehammer.

"What the devil's happening?"

"I don't know. The *Lepadus* was coming up astern. I thought she was going to ram us."

"We wouldn't be talking if she had. What happened before that? Why did we lose power?"

"I don't know. It was like we were being jammed."

"Precisely." Anya's cold, clipped voice was close at hand. "Such techniques are being perfected in the Soviet Union. That is why I had reservations concerning the conduct of this operation."

"You might express them a little more forcefully next time."

If there is going to be a next time, thought Bond. He heard the hiss of air as Carter activated the periscope and wondered why the sea had suddenly become so calm. They must be on the surface, and yet there was hardly any movement. Some men were holding up lighters, and the flames were steady. The only sound was that strange clanging noise. Bond felt the hairs on the back of his neck prickling.

"What can you see?"

"Nothing. I'm not getting anything. Blackout."

"Jesus Christ!" The voice came from one of the crew. Bond could sense the seeds of panic that would soon be spreading through the submarine. "What are we going to do, Captain? Open the hatch?"

Carter's voice was resolute. "Not until I know what the hell there is out there."

There was a violent explosion two feet behind Bond, and he instinctively ducked sideways. The hull of the submarine was humming. Whatever was happening out there was calculated to tear nerves to threads. Bond took a lighter and held it up to the hull. A cylindrical metal bolt had been fired through the side of the submarine. There was a small hole in its center. What did it all mean? Where were they?

"Captain, you have precisely two minutes to open your hatches and surrender your ship." The voice was muffled and must be coming through a limpet microphone attached to the side of the hull. Despite the distortion, the thin, measured tone was familiar. Stromberg. Bond saw Anya's eyes shining in the darkness. He read in them what he felt himself. Fear "The alternative is extermination by cyanide gas. We will pump the hull full of gas bolts if necessary. You will assemble your men on deck unarmed. Anyone found with a weapon or attempting to hide will be shot. You now have one and a half minutes."

Bond listened to men breathing in the darkness. A lighter went out. What alternatives were there? Escape via one of the torpedo tubes? No time. Gas masks? Useless against cyanide gas.

"You have one minute, Captain. Stand by to activate gas cylinders. Reload gas bolt."

Carter swore. "Bastards! They've got us over a barrel." He started to move toward the sail. There was a release of tension in the control room. Bond turned to Anya. "Keep your hair out of sight. Stromberg won't know we're aboard. We'll take our chance when we see what the set-up is."

Anya nodded and started to push her hair under her cap. The heat in the control room was unbearable. Bond wiped his dripping forehead with his sleeve and marvelled at the endurance of men who were prepared to stay below the surface for months at a time.

"So, living still appeals to you, Captain." Stromberg's voice crackled through the hull. "Very wise. Assemble your men immediately. There is little time left."

Carter appeared with a flashlight. He looked like a man hovering on the edge of reason. His face was hollow and drawn. "Okay, men, muster on the forward casing. Hurry it along." He turned to Bond but did not speak.

"Where are we?" said Bond.

Carter spoke as if finding it difficult to believe his own words. "We're inside the tanker."

"What?" Anya's long legs swept her toward the sail with Bond at her shoulder. Had Carter taken leave of his senses? Bond saw an oval of light above his head and pulled himself onto the navigation bridge. What he saw made his eyes widen in amazement. What had Carter's words been? "It's not possible!" The first impression was of being inside a cathedral—a huge space enclosed by walls and a vaulted ceiling far above. Pillars, columns, buttresses. The whole designed to throw the eye forward to a stained glass window radiating light which stretched from one wall to the other. Sepulchral shadows giving way to celestial incandescence. But this was no place of wor-

ship. On closer examination, the rood screen across the stained glass windows became louvered steel, shielding the face of a brilliantly lit control room. The columns became steel girders supporting gangways, gantries, and cat-walks, joined by flights of stairs and running both lengths of the structure and across its middle. Elevators served key access points to the galleries, and a tube-enclosed hovercar track with regular entry points ran beneath them. This was staggering enough, but it was only the beginning. Virtually the entire area bounded by the four walls was an enormous sea-filled dock divided by two jetties into three mooring bays. The nose of the *Wayne* was in the center bay, and on either side of her were two other submarines. Bond tried to keep pace with his amazement. As a conception it was more fantastic than anything he had ever seen or thought about. A vessel built in the guise of a tanker capable of swallowing submarines. And the two submarines already here? One British, one Russian. He tried to read the nameplates through the glare of the searchlights playing on his face.

"Hurry! I am not renowned for my patience." Again, Stromberg's hectoring voice. Bond climbed down the ladder to the deck wondering where it was coming from. On all sides, men with sub-machineguns were covering them from quay and gallery. A rubber tube, attached to the bolt that had been fired through the hull, ran from the side of the *Wayne* to one of a number of gas cylinders stacked on a trolley. Beside the man with his hand resting alertly on the gas cylinder was another, holding what looked like a pneumatic drill. This must be the gun for firing the gas bolts. The men wore the SS-and-fish insignia of the crew of the *Riva* and were dressed in the same blue uniform. Without exception they looked menacingly alert and well-trained. Bond's admiration for Stromberg increased in proportion to his fear and loathing. This man *was* capable of holding the world to ransom.

"That is the *Potemkin!*" Anya hissed the words as she moved beside Bond with her head down. Bond said nothing but looked beyond the steel pillar to the submarine in front of him. He could just make out the lettering

158

"—ger". *Ranger!* Thank God! But what about the crew? Had Stromberg murdered them? And here was the crew of the *Wayne* being lined up on the forward casing. What were they facing, a firing squad? Bond hesitated, wondering whether to spring at the nearest guard. But even if he wrested the man's weapon away he would be instantly gunned down from above. Best to wait and see. "Prisoners to brig."

Bond tucked his chin in and breathed a sigh of relief. They were not going to be killed—not yet, anyway. The guards gestured with the muzzles of their weapons, and the crew of the *Wayne* began to file down the gangway to the quayside. Bond looked ahead and saw three heavy steel doors in the bulkhead beneath the gallery that fronted the control room. There were two armed guards outside the doors and a cluster of disappointed faces showed through small square openings. "Why didn't you send the Marines?" said a Cockney voice.

Bond waited until he was out of view of the bridge beneath the wide gallery and looked back down the length of the interior of the *Lepadus*. It was obvious now why she had a straight rather than a bulbous bow. He could see the line that marked the closure point of the two huge doors. Once again, he marvelled at the enormity of the concept. To produce something of this size and intricacy must have cost countless millions of dollars. What did Stromberg hope to recoup from such an outlay? It must be more than mere money.

"Stop!" The voice echoed from the P.A. system like a rifle shot. The guards immediately thrust their weapons forward and the line of prisoners stumbled to a halt. Bond felt his heart miss a beat. What had happened? He glanced at Anya, but she was looking down into the oily waters of the dock.

"I believe we have unexpected guests. Guards, bring Mr. and Mrs. Sterling to the control room!" There was a deadly, mocking edge to the voice, and Bond's heart sank. How had they been spotted? And then he saw it, turning slowly along its track like an electric fan. Mounted on a rail sixty feet above their heads was a T.V. scanner relaying images back to the control room. A guard stepped into the ranks, and Bond recognized one of the men who had been at the laboratory. His face set into a mean leer, and he jabbed his automatic into Bond's stomach until the sight buried itself in flesh. *"Vas-y!"* Bond winced and resisted the temptation to brain the Corsican with his own weapon. Something told him he was going to need all the strength he had. Anya was plucked from the ranks and the two of them propelled toward a curved flight of stairs that led from the quayside to the control room. A torrent of jeers in Russian and English came from the grills along the brig. Bond noticed that the doors were secured by wheels like the door of a bank safe. At least the crews of the *Ranger* and *Potemkin* sounded as if they were spoiling for a fight. He only hoped he could provide them with one.

The flight of stairs ended outside the starboard side of the control room and Bond looked through the giant steel louvers that stood open like a procession of screens, the gap between each pair large enough to let a man walk through without turning his shoulders. The room was dominated by a twenty-foot-high globe, illuminated internally and revolving slowly. At various points on its surface, different-colored lights were flashing. Around the globe was a circular console manned by six technicians operating a galaxy of computers, print-out machines, and transmission units. Behind the globe was a long bank of closed-circuit television screens watched by a team of monitors. Bond smiled ruefully. No wonder they had been seen. There must be no part of the vessel that Stromberg could not keep under the minutest observation. The man left nothing to chance.

"Good day, Mr. Sterling—or perhaps we can dispense with pseudonyms—Commander Bond and Major Amasova." Stromberg rose from a revolving armchair set in front of the globe so that it provided a view of everything that was happening in the control room. He glided toward them with his strange ghostly walk, looking at first glance like a venerable mandarin in a black tunic. "You have arrived just in time. I am about to instigate Operation

160

Armageddon." Before Bond could speak, he turned aside and addressed a bearded man wearing the uniform of a merchant navy captain who was standing attentively in the entrance to the control room. "Proceed with launching, Captain."

"Yes, sir." The man turned on his heel and retired into the control room. Seconds later, his voice came over the P.A. system. "Attention, all personnel. Stromberg Crews One and Two—embark your submarines. Repeat—Crews One and Two—embark your submarines."

As Bond watched in amazement, the catwalks above the *Ranger* and *Potemkin* began to fill with men, and the whole structure drummed with the sound of moving feet. Down they filed like two columns of ants making for the submarines.

Bond looked at Anya. Her expression mirrored his puzzlement. Armageddon? The supreme conflict between nations. The end of the world?

A P.A. speaker crackled into life. "Both crews aboard, Captain. Missile onload completed." The hatch covers slid into place. The decks were smooth. The water glistened like the surface of a swimming pool.

Bond turned to Stromberg, who was looking down without expression.

"What does it all mean, Stromberg?"

Stromberg placed the tips of his fingers together in a gesture akin to prayer. He spoke softly. "The two submarines, generously donated by your respective governments, will shortly be putting to sea. They have been given their targets and by twelve noon they will have reached their firing positions. Shortly after twelve noon, New York and Moscow will cease to exist." He spoke in a precise, measured tone that was chilling. "I don't have to tell either of you what that means. Reprisals for what both great powers will take as a premeditated sneak attack will be immediate. Nuclear war on an unprecedented scale will break out. The world as we know it will be obliterated."

There was silence save for the lapping of water against the dockside. The Captain's voice came over the P.A. system. "Open bow doors." Bond gripped the rail before turning to face Stromberg. "All right. How much do you want?"

Stromberg's bland face was devoid of artifice. "Want, Commander Bond? What can *you* possibly give me?"

"Personally, very little." Bond tried to control his temper. "But those I represent—those Major Amasova represents . . . they can give you a great deal. Name your figure."

Stromberg shook his head as if not quite certain that he understood. "I think you are talking about money. I am not interested in money. I have all I need."

"Then what do you want?" Anya's tone was urgent. "Power? A seat on the Security Council? A world government under your control?"

Again there was silence broken by the Captain's voice over the P.A. system. "Stromberg One—proceed to sea. Stromberg Two—follow in line ahead."

Bond watched in horror as H.M.S. *Ranger* began to nose forward. "Yes, Stromberg! Name your terms. What do you want to call back those submarines?"

Stromberg turned slowly like a man in a trance and Bond found himself staring into eyes that were two long corridors leading nowhere. He realized then that Stromberg was completely and utterly mad. "You do not understand, Commander Bond. I *want* to destroy the world. I am going to create a new one."

Chapter 20

EXIT SIGMUND STROMBERG

"Create a new world?" Anya's voice was incredulous.

"Beneath the sea. Your friend"—Stromberg checked and pinched his small wet mouth into the semblance of a smile —"your colleague, Commander Bond, knows what I am talking about."

"I have no conception of what you're talking about!" Bond's voice blazed wtih anger. "If you want to start a colony on the ocean bed, start it! Why butcher countless millions of innocent people in the process?"

"They are not innocent!" Now it was Stromberg's turn to rage. "Do you ever look at the world you live in? Do you ever read a newspaper? Do you ever watch a television set? Corruption, betrayal, dishonesty, hate! These are the most prevalent human emotions. Society is hellbent on a course toward destruction. I am merely accelerating the process so that I can start a new and better civilization. I act not from malice, but from necessity."

"But how will the oceans fare in a nuclear war? The contamination will be immeasurably more severe."

The two departing submarines were now framed in the gaping bows of the *Lepadus*. It was like a painting. A painting of the end of the world.

"I disagree!" Stromberg's thin whine sang with mad menace.

"Better to end all at one stroke than continue with what we have now. I have made plans for all contingencies."

"You are mad," said Bond.

"I am not interested in your opinion." Stromberg's tone was withering. "I will accept the judgment of posterity."

"I can give it to you now," said Bond. "Sigmund Stromberg was the richest lunatic in history."

For a moment it seemed that there had been a subsidence of Stromberg's features. The mouth was sucked in on itself, and the eyes blazed with strange, ghastly fire. Then the spasm passed and the fluttering hands were still. "You seek to goad me, Commander Bond. But I am a scientist and a realist. I am above petty emotions. I, more than any man alive, have proved that I do not need to sink to the level of vulgar abuse!"

Bond listened to the megalomaniac "I's" tumbling from Stromberg's obscene little mouth and watched the huge bow doors begin to close. It was like being shut in a tomb. The submarines had departed to destroy the world, and he was left alone with a brilliant mind that had somehow become poisoned. Bond glanced toward the nearest guards. Both of them were alert and watching, their weapons in their hands. There was little chance of seizing a gun and holding Stromberg to ransom.

Stromberg beckoned to the guards. "And now, Commander, I must leave you. I am returning to my laboratory. You will stay here." He singled out Bond for the full force of that remark before turning to Anya. "You, Major, will accompany me. It may come as a surprise to you to learn that there is someone who awaits your presence with a palpitating eagerness and—may I say it?—no little tender feeling." Stromberg smiled cruelly. "Yes. My friend with the sophisticated masticatory apparatus, known in some circles as Jaws. In your brief meetings he has developed

164

a soft spot for you. Bizarre, is it not?" The revulsion on Bond's face was obvious. "I would not prejudge the match, Commander Bond. Even to a non-scientist the possibilities are fascinating. Beauty and great intelligence allied to ruthless cunning and phenomenal strength. The progeny of such a union should be remarkable."

Anya shuddered. "I would rather die."

Stromberg looked at her coldly. "That is certainly the only alternative." He gestured to one of the guards, who seized Anya roughly by the arm. She looked into Bond's eyes, and there was a hint of pleading together with a slackening of the tension around the proud mouth. She looked more like the girl he had held in his arms at the Hotel Carla di Volpe. He began to move forward, but the second guard was quick to read the message. His weapon swung up, and the sight dug into the side of Bond's neck beneath the jawbone. Bond could feel the man's finger taking up the play in the trigger. One false move, and the top of his head would be blown off.

"Spare us the schoolboy heroics, Commander Bond." Stromberg's tone was mocking, and Bond yearned to drive his fist into the cruel, contemptuous face and feel it crack like an egg. "Put him with the rest of the prisoners. The Captain has his instructions." Stromberg glanced down toward the canisters of cyanide gas that were being wheeled along the quay. "Farewell, Bond. The word has, I must say, a welcome ring of permanency about it."

Bond ignored Stromberg and tried to pump hope into Anya's apprehensive eyes. "*Au revoir*, Anya."

"Goodbye, James." There was no hatred in her voice. Perhaps a trace of resignation. A note of regret for missed opportunities. Bond watched her being led away and tried to purge his mind of sentiment. Why think of one girl when the future of the world hung in the balance? But what was the world except millions of girls like Anya? How could one serve humanity and ignore individuals? A door slid open to reveal an elevator, and Stromberg, Anya, and the guard stepped inside. Bond caught one last glimpse of Anya's brave, beautiful face staring at him impassively, and then the door slid shut.

165

"Move!"

The barrel of the automatic was thrust into Bond's neck and then pulled back as the guard covered him warily. Bond began to move toward the stairs by which he had approached the control room. Behind him, he could hear the typewriter chatter of the print-out machines and the babble of the technicians. Above, the scanner continued to move slowly along its programmed path. Guards were stationed at regular intervals along all gangways and catwalks. Bond knew that if he was going to do something, he had to do it fast. If two hundred and fifty men had found it impossible to escape from the brig, his presence amongst them was not going to change things in the short term—and it was a short term. Just a few hours, and the submarines would be in position. He had to get inside that control room!

Now they were at the bottom of the stairs and beginning to move along the quay. The two guards outside the first door of the brig looked up expectantly. A third man was approaching with the trolley load of gas canisters. On top of them rested the bolt gun. Bond tensed and felt a sharp stab of excitement. Would it still be loaded? How could he lay hands on it? The trolley was of a simple construction, one upright slotted in at each corner. If one of them was dislodged, the canisters would come tumbling down. Bond licked his dry lips. The two guards outside the brig had their automatics slung around their shoulders. The trolley was twenty feet away. Bond turned, and the guard gestured at him to keep moving. He was five feet behind. Right. This was it. Bond tensed his thigh and braced his toes inside his steel-capped parachute boots. Ten feet, five feet. Bond slowed as if to let the trolley past and then—"*Yumf!*" The exclamation burst from Bond's lips as he lashed out at the underside of the trolley with all his strength.

The boot crunched against the upright and pain ricocheted through his leg. The upright jolted into the air and the first canister came crashing down. Before it had touched the deck, Bond had snatched up the bolt gun and back-chopped the trolley guard into the water. Canisters were spilling everywhere, and he heard the first guard

166

stumble as they rained down about his ankles. He ducked and started running toward the farthest door of the brig. A burst of automatic fire streamed over his head like angry wasps, and he darted behind a stanchion. The two warders had unslung their weapons and were coming for him. Behind, the first guard angled for a target.

A machine gun started chattering from the central catwalk, and bullets screamed off the metal plating above Bond's head. The unexpected intervention distracted the quayside attackers and Bond sprang out, struggling to level the heavy bolt gun. He pulled the trigger and was hurled backwards by the recoil. With sickening force, the bolt tore through the first warder as if he was a box of wet tissues and then entered the body of the second, chewing and spewing its way through bone and gristle until it stood a hideous six inches beyond his back. Like severed puppets the men buckled at the knees and followed each other to the deck in a gushing fountain of blood. Bond threw himself forward and snatched up the first man's automatic. He found the trigger and rolled sideways as bullets spattered the area in front of him.

Stromberg's guard was now out in the open, his face a mask of desperation and hate. Bond aimed at the knees and worked upwards. Life went out of the man and he slumped forward with enough force to send his automatic sliding ten feet across the deck. Bond rolled again and ran, stooped, for the nearest door of the brig. He fired a defiant burst toward the central gangway and began to wrench at the wheel. Its progress was slow at first, but then it began to spin. A sudden sharp pain in his upper arm told him that he had been hit. He spun around and saw a man taking aim from a fin of the *Wayne*. He fired a short burst and the man flopped onto the deck and then slowly slid into the water. Back to the wheel. God damn it! How many turns did it take to open it? Bullets were homing in from all sides.

"Come on! Come on!" The voices urging him on came from behind the door as well as inside his mind. He could feel their shoulders pressing against it. Then he was thrust backwards. A surge of bodies welled out onto the quayside.

Carter was kneeling beside him. "Thank God, Bond! I'll get you a Medal of Merit for this."

"I've already turned one down." Bond's voice changed gear into action immediately. "You take charge down here. I've got to get up on deck. Stromberg's taking off with Anya. We need to get inside that control room."

He was running before Carter had time to nod. Bullets were spraying like lead confetti. A concentration of fire was being directed at the men spilling from the brig, and they had only three weapons to reply with. Correction, four. Bond levelled his automatic at a man firing from the gallery and he sagged forward, relinquishing his weapon to the grateful horde fanning out behind any cover that presented itself.

Bond dropped his shoulder and charged through an oval metal door as bullets skipped at his heels. A flight of stairs zigzagged upward. Now it was just the sound of his boots ringing against the metal as he headed for the deck. Blood was slopping down the inside of his sleeve, but his arm was still functioning. Within him was a deadly sense of purpose that kept him going. He must eliminate Stromberg. With its brains destroyed, perhaps the monster would slither to a halt. The submarine commanders would listen to reason; Armageddon could be avoided.

Bond felt fresh air beating against his face. He must be near the deck. The sinews of his legs screamed for respite. He urged himself forward and fell against the heavy handle that twisted downward to give him access to the deck. My God! Where was he? Bond stuck his head out of the deck housing and felt a small gale tugging at his head. He might be on the roof of a gigantic building. Miles of pipes ran into infinity like railway lines across an endless plain. The sky lowered down as if feeling menaced by the brute structure soaring up beneath it.

Bond heard the developing roar of rotor blades and jerked his head toward the Bavarian madness of the stern. Silhouetted against the towering bridge structure was the Bell, lifting into the air. Bond started to run toward it, jumping over pipes until he came to the central catwalk.

He sprang onto a hatch cover and clawed his way up,

throwing the automatic in front of him. Now he had it in his grasp and was rising to his feet. The helicopter stabilized, tipped, and began to follow the line of the catwalk as if using it as a runway. Bond could see its glinting, bulbous nose, like the head of a dragonfly, getting larger and larger. All he had to do was raise his gun and rake it from nose to tail as it flew overhead. He tensed, seeing the outlines of the pilot and Stromberg and—Anya. The vibrating roar filled Bond's ears. His finger tightened against the trigger. The helicopter filled the sky above his head. He waited for the sound of the bullets ripping into the fuselage, the cockpit exploding like a lightbulb. Nothing. Nothing at all. His finger trembled against the trigger as if in a death spasm. Nothing happened. The surface-thumping beat of the rotor blades began to die away. Bond spun around. The helicopter was rising now, clearing the bow of the *Lepadus* and tilting away to starboard. It looked incredibly small against the landing field specifications of the tanker's deck.

With a sense of shame that was physically painful, Bond realized what he had done. He had betrayed his country and himself because of his attachment to a woman. He had not opened fire because Anya was a prisoner in the cockpit. What a contemptible fool he was! Bitter and self-despising, he turned his back on the spectacle of his perfidy.

Like a Quixotic windmill, the bridge soared into the air before him. Right! Pull yourself together, Bond! Attack! He started to run down the catwalk toward the helideck. Two mechanics and a guard were moving cans away from its perimeter. Refueling must have been done by hand. Bond opened up from long range and corrected his aim according to the passage of his bullets. A fuel can exploded and, instantly, the helideck was a square pool of flame. Aviation fuel had been slopped all over it. A yellow flame soared into the sky, its edge shimmering so that the bridge seemed to be seen through plastic. Tongues of red ran through the flame, and a man staggered out of it like a blazing torch. As Bond watched, he appeared to dissolve into the deck. The heat singed Bond's eyelashes and

169

scorched his cheeks. There was no air left to breathe. The roar of the flames was deafening. Bond fell back as there was a second explosion, more powerful than the first. The rest of the fuel cans had gone up. Now the yellow became embroidered with needles of black, and a dense smoke blotted out the bridge. One of the oil tanks next to the cofferdam must have caught fire.

Bond scrambled over the rail of the catwalk and dropped to the deck. The fire would cause a valuable diversion. He broke into a run and hurdled the pipes that blocked his path to the nearest deck housing. Now the mist of self-loathing was clearing, and he could reprogram his mind to the job in hand. Get inside the control room! That was the most important objective. He clattered down the stairs as a guard loomed out of a companionway beside him. Bond pressed the trigger, but the magazine was empty. The man spun to fire but Bond knocked the weapon sideways and drove the barrel of his gun into the unprotected stomach. The man jackknifed and Bond swung the butt of his weapon in a vicious, two-handed uppercut that delivered the forged steel flush to the side of the jaw. The neck snapped like a stick of rock. Bond unclamped the dead fingers, one by one, and took the man's weapon. He slung his own over his shoulder and continued down the stairs.

As he approached the bottom, he could hear the steady drumming of automatic fire. The battle was not over. He waited behind the heavy metal door and listened to his heart pounding. The blood was coagulating about his wrist and the arm was stiffening up. He could not afford to stop moving. Taking several deep breaths, he twisted the handle and leaned against the door sufficiently to push it open a couple of inches. The murky water glimmered in front of him. As he had imagined, he was farther down toward the bows than when he had entered the port companionway. Above him and toward the stern was the central catwalk that traversed the dock area. In its middle was a revolving gun platform now facing toward the brig. Bond could see the backs of the three gunners as they crouched behind the shield. He looked toward the control room, and his heart fell. The louvers were shut tight to form an impenetrable wall. Half a dozen bodies lay scattered on the balcony in front of them.

It was brutally clear that there was no easy way through to the nerve center of the Stromberg empire. And there were less than four hours to Armageddon.

Chapter 21

DROWNED, BURIED AND CREMATED . . .

Bond fought off weariness and despondency and edged his way out onto the quayside. There had never been any doubt that it was going to be difficult. Once you started feeling sorry for yourself, you were finished. Maybe the same was true about feeling sorry for other people.

He shrank back against the iron plating and reviewed the situation. From what he could see, Carter and the rest of the escaped prisoners were spread out around the berths. Some of them had gotten into the side galleries; occasional shots were winging from that direction. A number of them had perished in an unsuccessful attack on the control room. From the spread of their fire it sounded as if they had laid hands on some more weapons. But wherever they moved, they were within range of the central gun emplacement on the catwalk. That had to be knocked out. Bond's eye swung on a closer orbit. The hovercar track and its protective tube ran within six feet. One of the hovercraft was conveniently placed in the nearest opening. That was twenty feet away. Bond looked around him and emerged from the shadow.

172

He had taken two steps when there was an ear-splitting screech above his head. He threw himself full length and screwed his eyes shut, waiting for the bullets to skewer into his flesh. Nothing happened. The siren continued to wail and he relaxed fractionally. It must be an alarm signal announcing the fire on deck. No help likely from down here, chums. They've all got their hands full. He raised his head and crawled toward the hovercar. It was a simple six-seater shell with a dead-man's-handle connecting to the electrified monorail. Lift it and you got the juice to propel the hovercar. The wailing of the siren stopped and there was an eerie silence broken by the groans of a wounded man lying near the brig. There was a short burst of fire from the central catwalk, and the groans stopped. Bond's teeth ground together with a sound that was almost audible. He didn't like shooting people in the back but sometimes they made it easier for you.

Looking carefully along the gallery that ran above his head, he straightened up and peered across to the far gallery. There was no sign of movement. Now he had to move fast before his own side picked him out as one of the enemy and started shooting. He unslung his empty weapon and placed it in the cockpit of the hovercar. Then he scrambled onto the roof of the track cover and moved toward the bows. Ten paces and he was beyond the gun crew. Looking up, he could see their shoulders hunched behind the square metal plate with the observation slits. He raised his gun and there was a warning shout followed by a burst of automatic fire from the shadows opposite. Bond concentrated on the gun crew. As they spun around he unleashed a long burst and saw two of the men buckle and slump. The third was struggling with the handle that turned the gun. Bond fired again, but the defensive shield continued to swing around. He could see the sparks as his bullets screamed off it. The gun barrels were depressing toward him when the third man suddenly slid sideways and lay still with his arm draped over one of the gantry rails.

Bond could feel his body awash with sweat. The tunnel beneath his feet was raked by bullets, and he started to run toward the hovercar. He sprang through the opening and snatched at the lever. There was a high-pitched whine, and the hovercar lifted and began to glide forward. Bullets drummed against the tunnel housing like tropical rain. Bond kept his head down and the handle up. Two more openings flashed by, and he was at the quayside on the port side of the brig. He saw the startled faces of Carter's men bringing their weapons to bear. "Hold your fire, men!" Bond felt a surge of gratitude for Carter's quick reading of the situation and scrambled out to shelter behind the stairs leading up to the control room. Carter ducked down beside him. "Did you get him?"

"No."

Carter noticed from the expression on Bond's face that something was wrong, but he did not pursue it. "Tough. Thanks for knocking out that machine gun. We got the guy who was trying to nail you. I think we've just about cleaned them up out here, but they're thick as ticks on a hog's back in that control room."

Bond saw that Carter was holding an FN automatic rifle. "Where did that come from?"

"We got into the magazine. We've got no problems about arms."

"Excellent." Bond looked through the door of the brig where he could see Chuck Coyle supervising the treatment of a line of injured men. Dead bodies lay where they had dropped. The ghastly stench of death already filled the air. "What about losses?"

Carter's face clouded. "Heavy. They really poured it into us coming out of the brig. About thirty dead and half as many again injured. The Russian Captain bought it in the assault on the magazine." Carter shook his head in admiration. "Those guys fought like wildcats."

"What about Talbot, your opposite number on *Ranger?*"

"He's over there behind the other stairway. He's itching to have a go at the control room. He thinks he can blast his way in with hand grenades."

Bond thought about the four-inch-thick steel louvers and was skeptical. He looked at his watch. Three and a half hours to go. "Let's have a talk with him."

Talbot was in his mid-thirties, blond-haired and handsome in a typically English way which made his face seem unmarked by any contact with the cruder aspects of life. Bond could imagine the teacups at the vicarage trembling when he returned on leave.

"Absolutely. My chaps are rearing at the bit. Give us some covering fire and we'll be in there like a dose of salts."

Bond felt uneasy, but with every second that passed, the two nuclear submarines were drawing closer to their firing positions. Something had to be done. He turned from Talbot's eager, shiny face and read the resignation in Carter's tired, red-veined eyes.

"All right."

Five minutes later, Talbot was poised beneath the shelter of the gallery with twenty men. They were armed with Schmeisser sub-machineguns found in the magazine and four hand grenades wrapped in cloth so that they could be lobbed against the foot of the metal screen without rolling away.

The assault party was divided into two groups of ten. They would attack simultaneously up the two stairways, under covering fire from the side of the quay. Covering fire against what? thought Bond as he looked toward the blank wall of steel. He had a terrible sense of foreboding but tried to shut it out of his mind.

Talbot swung his arm from side to side to show that he was ready and machine-gun fire began to rake the steel louvers. There was the nerve-torturing screech of bullets glancing off metal but no suggestion that any impression was being made. The louvers remained bland and impervious as closed eyes. Then, suddenly, the eyes opened. Talbot's shouting men had reached the top of the stairways when four vertical slits appeared in the steel curtains and the cheese-grater barrels of heavy machine guns poked into view.

Bond winced and prepared for the inevitable. The barrels shuddered and a hail of bullets cut a swathe through the attackers. The muzzle velocity was so great that men seemed to be wiped away like figures from a blackboard. One, more in advance of the others, was held in the air by the weight of bullets pouring into him. He trembled as if a powerful hosepipe was playing on his chest and then pitched full length. Bond felt like weeping as he watched his countrymen being butchered. Only Talbot remained to charge on, firing from the hip. He lobbed his hand grenade and then staggered after it like a bowler following through his delivery. Two faltering steps and a thin column of flame burst from an opening in the louvers and engulfed him. Within seconds he was a blazing torch collapsing on his own grenade. There was an explosion and he was tossed in the air like a theatrical prop. Pieces of burning uniform lay scattered across the deck. The steel louvers were unscathed. As if performing a drill movement, the gun barrels withdrew at the same instant and the slits closed. Dying men twitched and the disgusting roast pork smell of burning flesh began to waft down from the gallery. Bond felt sick in mind and body.

"Oh, my God!" Carter's eyes were closed.

"Right." Bond fought to retain his composure and do something positive. "That taught us a lesson. No conventional small-arm is going to get us into that place. What else is there in the magazine?"

Carter wiped his grimy forehead across his sleeve and blinked. He was like a boxer shaking off a painful blow, knowing that the fight had to continue. "Torpedoes. They took them all out and checked them over. Nuclear and conventional." Bond found the grain of an idea beginning to form itself at the back of his mind. "Can you lay your hands on an armorer?" Carter looked around the men huddled disconsolately behind any protection that presented itself. "I sure hope so. Why?"

Bond squared his jaw. "I want to build a bomb."

One and a half hours later, Bond stood in the magazine feeling like a surgeon presiding over a life-or-death operation. On the armorer's table was the dismembered shell of a conventional torpedo and around it a complicated mass of colored wires and electrical circuits. Two men bent over the "patient" and another stood by to wipe the sweat from their foreheads. It was not only the sweat of fear but a result of the intense heat that was building up in the magazine. Three explosions of increasing severity had rocked the tanker in the last hour, and Bond assumed that these were results of the fire he had left blazing on deck. The bulkheads were becoming hot to the touch, and it was possible that the fire was spreading through the ship. Drowned, buried, and cremated. That would add color to his discreet obituary in the *Times*.

"How's it going?" Bond found it agonizing to be denied physical involvement.

"Nearly there, sir." The voice was calm, controlled and comforting. "We just want to make sure we don't touch the impulse conductor circuit."

Bond swallowed the vacuum in his throat. "Supposing you do?"

"Well, sir"—the voice was apologetic—"it might go off."

Bond cursed himself for asking and tried to think of something else. What, for instance—it was of course purely accident that she had swum so readily into his mind—what was happening to Anya?

"I am sorry." Nobody hearing Stromberg's voice could have doubted its sincerity. "But you do have a distressing tendency toward violence that must be controlled. The manacles will be removed when you demonstrate a more rational attitude toward your new situation. I wish you could be reasonable. You are exceptionally favored. You, above all others, have been selected as the initiator of a new civilization. You are akin to Mary in the Christian dogma. Does not the significance of that mean something to you? Plucked from nothing to be the womb that furnishes an original species?" His gaze drifted sideways to light upon the nail-raked cheek of Jaws, the dark blood wrinkling as it dried in its short-run tributaries.

Anya looked up and saw the stoked fires behind the glazed, pig eyes. The lips beginning to furl back from the ghastly, robot mouth. Oh God, she prayed, do not let him kiss me again.

"We're there, sir."

Bond stepped forward to see the detonator being drawn away gently from its wires. He breathed an audible sigh of relief. "I'd clap you on the back if I wasn't frightened of blowing us all to kingdom come. What fuses have we got?"

"Twelve seconds, sir."

Bond watched the small bags of explosive being packed tightly around the detonator and raised his eyes to Carter on the other side of the table. If he read the expression right, it said: if this doesn't work, we're done for.

Chapter 22

FIVE MINUTES TO ARMAGEDDON

Bond clung to the steel girder and fought the waves of tiredness and nausea that passed through him. His shoulder was throbbing painfully. Sixty feet below, the water of the dock glinted dully. If he fell, he would land on the starboard diving plane of the *Wayne*. Pray God that his arm held out. He raised himself up so that he straddled the girder and winced as the metal cut into his thighs. Another wave of dizziness made him close his eyes and cling like a limpet until he was sure that he had his balance. He breathed naturally until his heart stopped thumping and then began to ease the straps of the haversack off his shoulders. More balancing problems. The pack was heavy. Eventually, he was able to swing it around with both hands and place it on the girder in front of him. A corner of the flap gaped open and revealed the thin pencil fuse. He conquered his vertigo and looked back toward the central catwalk. Running on its rail beneath the girder, the T.V. scanner was gliding toward him. It turned slowly from side to side like some ugly, all-seeing insect eye.

179

Bond let it pass beneath him and judged the distance to the heavy metal arm that held it to the rail. It moved on with a slight clanking noise and approached the center point of the louvered screen of the control room. Bond raised his left wrist and looked at his watch. One . . . two . . . three . . . the seconds ticked by and Bond measured the progress of the scanner on its return journey. When twelve seconds had passed he knew exactly where the scanner would be on its rail; approximately fifteen feet from the louvers. He let the scanner pass beneath him and began to edge forward along the girder. Now his heart was thumping uncontrollably and the palms of his hands were wet. If anyone peered through the weapon slits in the louvers they must see him. He was, literally, a sitting target.

He reached the point he had marked with his eye and leaned forward to seize the haversack by the crudely fashioned S-shape hook that had been attached to its back. Another wave of nausea swept over him. Behind, the scanner reached the end of its track and obediently swung around with the now familiar clanking noise. Half a minute and it would be beneath him. He was now nearly over the balcony and he could see Carter and his men crouching at the foot of the stairways. God lend him strength to provide them with a better chance than poor Talbot had been given. He turned his head with difficulty and saw that the scanner was now twenty feet away. Gritting his teeth, he lay at full stretch with his head turned to one side and his cheek pressed against the girder. His arms stretched down on either side, and he clutched the haversack with both hands and waited.

Boom!

The force of the explosion rocked the ship, the lights flickered, and the scanner stopped. Bond clung to his perch by his toenails and nearly cried out in pain and exasperation. The scanner was four feet from his reach. The weight of the bomb was tearing his injured arm out its socket. He could not hold it for more than a few seconds. If the latest explosion had affected the power supply, they were finished. Come on, damn you! He bit his lip and

180

tasted blood. His fingers slowly started to open. If he dropped the bomb on the quayside and it went off . . . the thought gave him the strength to lock his fingers. He could feel the sinews of his arms being systematically torn from their mooring. And then the lights flickered and the scanner clanked into action. Bond forced his head away from the girder and closed a numb finger and thumb around the fuse. He pressed without feeling anything and aimed the hook at the scanner arm. His first thrust was brushed aside but he launched himself forward and nearly rolled off the girder in a desperate effort to keep up with it. The hook scored the flesh on the back of his hand and then twisted around the scanner arm. The haversack dropped and then hung trembling behind the scanner as it joggled away.

As if hypnotized, Bond watched it narrowing the distance to the steel wall. And then the voice of self-preservation shouted in his ear. He thrust himself backwards in a series of untidy leapfrogs and then, when the scanner seemed to be almost against the louvers, twisted around, and threw himself in a despairing leap toward the dock. He missed the quayside by inches and hit the water as a blinding flash and a thunderclap of noise reverberated through the ship. The water closed above his head, and when he came up it was to see a thick pall of smoke spilling over the balcony and hear the rattle of small-arms fire.

Willing hands pulled him from the water, and he snatched up an automatic and drove his legs toward the starboard staircase. His head rose above the level of the gallery and he saw that the central louvers had been blasted out of true. They looked like blackened, crooked teeth. A giant hole had been torn in the metal screen.

Bond ran through the smoke to find that the battle was over. Those of Stromberg's men who had not been killed were being herded into a corner and made to lie face down with their hands behind their heads. A few technicians still cowered beside their machines. With a certain grim satisfaction, Bond saw that no quarter had been given. Each of the machine-gunners was dead at his post. He was relieved to find Carter striding toward him.

"Make that a Congressional Medal of Honor."

Bond tried to smile. "Where's the Captain?"

Carter nodded toward the giant globe, which was still turning on its axis. "If he's not dead, he soon will be."

Bond found the man lying with the front of his uniform soaked in blood. The color contrasted with the deathly pallor of his face. He raised his head defiantly. "You are too late. Our submarines are already on station. In five minutes they will launch their missiles." He shook his head. "There is nothing you can do."

Bond turned away. He was tired almost to death. His wound had reopened and all he wanted to do was to lie down and be allowed to go to sleep. But that was impossible. He had to think—and he had to think fast. Less than five minutes. What the hell were they going to do? His eyes sped over the banks of equipment trying to find a solution. Then he saw something. It was a chance. A faint chance. But it was all they had.

One of the relay screens on the console showed a set of coordinates. Bond looked from them to the giant globe. Two lights, marked "S1" and "S2," flashed from positions in the Atlantic. Stromberg One and Stromberg Two. *Ranger* and *Potemkin!* Bond checked the positions on the globe against the coordinates on the relay screen. The position of the *Potemkin* approximated that on the screen. Now, where were the coordinates of *Ranger*?

Another explosion thundered through the ship, and a slight list to starboard became more pronounced. Black smoke was pouring out of one of the ventilator fans. Bond could feel the seconds ticking away with every tortured heartbeat. Carter was looking into his face imploringly. "James—"

Bond held up his hand and looked at his watch. "I know. We have four minutes. Can you work a print-out transmission unit?"

"Sure. Why?"

"Find one and get ready to transmit. I'll tell you in a moment."

Bond's eyes ranged to the opposite aisle of the console. A body was slumped across one of the machines. He pulled it aside, and his heart lifted. Through a smear of

182

blood he could make out the faint, flickering digitals of another set of coordinates. He checked them off against the globe, and they approximated the indicated position of *Ranger*. Running to Carter's side, he flicked up the switch marked "Stromberg One." Carter looked up at him, strained and puzzled. Bond took a deep breath. "We're going to try to re-target those submarines."

"What on?"

"Each other." Bond did not pause for a reaction to his words.

"I'm going to give you *Potemkin*'s position as a target for *Ranger*—"

"And vice versa." Carter's face lit up. "My God! It might just work." His fingers were poised over the keys, and Bond started reeling out the figures. Below him, the message that might save the world began to take shape like a business telex. "Message to Captain of Stromberg One. New target coordinates. Repeat, new target coordinates—"

In less than a minute it was done, and Carter started to contact *Potemkin*. Supposing the two submarines were in communication with each other? Bond shivered. The whole plan was built on "if's." He watched the telex machine. At one minute to midday it chattered into life.

"Stromberg One. Message received and understood."

Carter sighed in relief and snapped his finger.

"Come on, Stromberg Two, talk to daddy."

Bond turned to the globe and looked at the throbbing lights indicating New York and Moscow. People waking, people sleeping—perhaps, soon, people dying.

"James!"

The telex was working again. "Stromberg Two. Message received and understood." It was exactly twelve o'clock.

Bond slumped into a chair and faced the slowly turning globe. Now that the die was cast, he felt strangely calm. Whatever more might have been expected of him, he had done all that he could. He would have liked a drink. A large dry martini with the thinnest sliver of freshly pared lemon peel.

"Look, James!"

Something was happening on the globe. Two dotted lines of lights were rising from the submarine symbols. Bond stiffened. These must be tracing the paths of the missiles. The dotted line from the South Atlantic seemed to be travelling toward New York. The line from the north was rising as if about to veer eastward. What had happened? Had the captains ignored the change of coordinates? Fear drove a wedge into his heart. Then a pattern began to establish itself. The missiles were travelling in an arc. They rose and then began, slowly but remorselessly, to veer toward each other. The traces overlapped, and one bisected the other as they started to descend. Bond watched, fascinated, as the dotted lines drew nearer and nearer to "S1" and "S2." Behind, the tanker listed and groaned, playing out a minor drama of its own. It was like watching an enormous firework fuse burn down. The globe spun once more, and when it came around there were no dotted lines, no symbols.

"Jesus Christ!" said Carter. "I think we've done it."

An explosion punctuated his words, and Bond pulled himself to his feet. It wasn't over yet. "Now we save ourselves. What's the situation on deck?"

"We can't get up there." Coyle had appeared at their side, his face black with smoke and oil. "It's a sheet of flame from bow to stern. The companionways are buckling with the heat."

"We'll have to go out the way we came in," said Carter. "Get everybody aboard the *Wayne* and get those bow doors open. Stromberg's men have last priority. We're going to be like sardines as it is."

"Yes, sir!" Coyle turned away and started bellowing through a loud hailer.

Bond looked around for a radio. "We must tell the outside world what's happening. Those two submarines going up are going to put everybody on nuclear alert. God knows how much damage has been caused."

Carter nodded grimly. "Okay, I'll supervise embarkation. Don't leave it too late!" He had to shout the last words as there was a staccato ripple of explosions, and flames belched out of one of the ventilator grills. The

184

paint on the forward bulkhead was blistering. Bond groped his way through the smoke and found a VHF set. It was hot to the touch. He began to transmit the special call sign, which should immediately be picked up by the nearest area station of Universal Export. Lights were beginning to go out and generators whine down into unnerving silence. Come on, you lazy bastards! What are you doing? Listening to the ice cubes clinking in your gin and tonics?

"Station Y. State your message. Over."

Thank God! Bond hunched over the speaker. "On no account implement Red Revenge. Repeat. On no account implement Red Revenge. Explanation will follow. 007 for London. Out."

Bond left the voice asking for further information and started to run toward the gallery. Heat and smoke were now turning the control room into a death chamber. The tanker was listing hard to starboard. It was difficult to keep his feet.

A violent explosion racked the control room and hurled Bond to the deck. The giant globe crashed onto the console and disintegrated. Severed wires spluttered angrily in the smoke-filled darkness. Bond started to claw his way to his feet and winced as a fragment of broken glass cut him to the bone.

"James?" Carter nearly fell over him before seizing his arm and dragging him toward the gap in the louvers. "The bow doors won't open. We'll have to blast our way out!"

Bond stumbled onto the gallery and peered through the smoke toward the dock. Water had risen fast and the starboard side of the quay was submerged. The bows of the *Wayne* swung free and men were swimming to reach the forward hatch. The area around her was crowded with crew members of the British, American, and Russian submarines trying to help their wounded comrades aboard. Stromberg's men were being held back at gunpoint. It was a scene of desperation and confusion that bordered on panic. Smoke, flames, and the smell of battle and burning flesh. Injured men who were frightened of being left behind were crying out and trying to drag themselves

185

toward the *Wayne*. Others were struggling to keep clear of the rising water.

Bond found one of Talbot's men who was still alive and began to help him down the stairs. Below him, he saw two rats swim through the water and scramble onto a floating corpse. This was a hell by Hieronymus Bosch. Was this degrading slaughter what Stromberg had in mind when he planned the end of the world? Bond reached the bottom of the stairs and water swirled over his feet. The man in his arms was babbling incoherently and beginning to falter. Bond fought to keep his feet. Another explosion rocked the tanker, and the list became more pronounced. The water was now up to his waist and running wild as if fretting to be free of its metal bonds. Into the brig it swirled, snatching up the relics of the last six hours of bitter struggle and battering them against the steel walls. The lights were going out one by one and the smoke was lowering down upon the stygian gloom. Bond remembered the obituary he had written for himself earlier—"drowned, burned, and buried." With every second, the type became more readable. Keeping close hold on the man in his arms, he advanced precariously toward the invisible quayside. The last berthing ropes of the *Wayne* had been slipped, and she now rode free of the sunken jetty. Carter had scrambled onto the stern and was looking back.

Another list, and Bond felt the deck lurching away beneath him. He scrabbled like a skier trying to find an edge on a steep slope and then lost his footing completely. He trod water for an instant and then sank until he felt a firm surface beneath his feet. Bracing himself, he drove off it and surged through the water like a swimmer starting a backstroke race. The survivor of Talbot's raid was still keeping him unconscious company. Bond's shoulders smacked against the side of the *Wayne* and strong hands snapped into the collar of his tunic. He was hauled up the side of the pear-drop hull and relinquished his grip on his countryman only when he saw that he was securely held by members of the *Wayne*'s crew.

"Get 'em below!" Carter disappeared through the main access hatch and Bond struggled to his feet and followed him. Below, it was like a crowd scene from an Eisenstein film. Men were pressed shoulder to shoulder, and the wounded found space between their feet. Carter fought his way to the control room and barked into the P.A. system. "All personnel below decks. Close hatches. Diving stations."

Bond's glazed eyes stared at the crowded metal walls pressing in on him and wondered if he had not exchanged a tomb for a coffin.

"All personnel aboard, sir"—there was an unhappy pause—"all that are left, that is. Hatches shut and clipped. Submarine ready for sea."

Carter's lips trembled, and then he spoke urgently. "Torpedo room—control. Load tube one with Mark 46 torpedo. Engine room—control. Hold her steady."

Bond looked at the faces about him. The sweat poured from them. The tension showed on each death-haunted feature.

"Torpedo room—control. Open outer door on tube one."

A man closed his eyes and his lips began to murmur a prayer.

"Control—torpedo room. Outer door on tube one open." The voice came from Texas. It was unwavering. Something—or someone—thumped against the side of the hull. Carter's fist clenched.

"Match bearings and shoot."

The man who was praying pressed a thin gold crucifix between finger and thumb. Bond noticed that the indentation on its transversals had been worn smooth. Two voices spoke out from the back of the control room.

"Set."

"Shoot!"

The *Wayne* shuddered and Bond tensed. There was the passage of seconds and then a giant swell buffeted the submarine. The bows pitched into the air and men clung to any support that offered itself. Bond watched the deck tilt up in front of him and heard wounded men cry out in pain and panic as they were trampled under foot. Almost instantly, a second shock wave hit the *Wayne*, as the back-surge rebounded from the quay. Bond crashed into Carter's back, and the two men sprawled across the deck. Carter was on his feet first and brought the periscope hissing from the well. His hands snapped on the handles and his back arched. When he turned away, his face showed a grim triumph close to tears. He nodded to Bond.

"Take a look."

Bond pressed his eyes to the viewer. Ahead, the great doors tilted like lopsided bookends. A jagged bite mark showed where the torpedo had blasted a way through them. Bond could see the sky beyond. Behind him, Carter's voice rang out triumphantly.

"Take her out!"

Chapter 23

COMING UP FOR AIR

"Well?" said Bond.

Carter tapped the piece of paper in his hand. "The order's been confirmed by Washington. 'Destroy Stromberg's laboratory with all possible speed.'"

Bond looked skeptical. "If it's still there. I told you, it's not attached to the sea bed. It can be moved."

Carter frowned, sensing the unfamiliar lack of enthusiasm in Bond's voice. "It was still there an hour ago. I've had an aerial reconnaissance report. No sign of life. No helicopter, either."

"They must have pulled out." Was Bond wrong, or did he actually feel relieved that Anya might not be on Atlantis? "How are you going to destroy it?"

"Torpedoes. If the layout is as you describe it, we'll blast it through the opening in the caldera. Officially, it will be a spontaneous eruption of what was thought to be an extinct volcano. The Italian Navy will move in and close the area. Their government has been informed."

"Very neat."

"What's the matter, James? You're not exactly bursting with enthusiasm. Don't you want to get Stromberg?"

Bond pulled himself together. "Of course I do. I just want to ask you one favor. Before you destroy Atlantis, I'd like the chance to get aboard by myself."

Carter jerked his head heavenward in a gesture of exasperation.

"Hell, James! Are you mad? I told you my orders. *'Destroy Atlantis with all possible speed.'* That didn't come from the Sweetbrush P.T.A."

"An hour." Bond's voice was calm, but it had a hard edge to it. "I'm I'm not back within an hour, you can send the whole hellish structure to the bottom."

Carter's reply veiled his concern for Bond. "You're trying to get me court-martialled, James."

Bond's face did not lighten. The tone remained firm. There was no hint of supplication. "An hour. That's all I need." Carter looked into the hard gunmetal eyes seared with red lines of pain and fatigue. "What is it, James? Stromberg, or the girl?" The tight, cruel line of Bond's mouth divided like a trap being sprung. "Let's say both."

Bond never discovered the speed they made through the Straits of Gibraltar and past the Balearics, but he estimated that it must be in excess of forty knots. He was, however, able to catch up on some important items of world news over the ship's radio. A mysterious tidal wave had lashed the west coast of Ireland, causing considerable damage but mercifully few deaths. A number of ships had been lost. A similar natural phenomenon in the area of the Windward Islands had savaged the east coast of Barbados and caused widespread damage in the islands of St. Lucia, Martinique, and Dominica. Both disturbances were said to be the results of seismic eruptions on the ocean bed and demonstrated that when it stirred itself, nature could reproduce a cataclysm of almost man-made proportions. Bond wondered drily whether informed scientific opinion would be able to link these eruptions with that which was shortly going to take place off the coast of northeast Sardinia. Amongst natural disasters of this magnitude, a report of the sinking of one of the world's largest and newest tankers, the *Lepadus*, was hardly given news space. Bond knew that the sight of the great iron coffin sliding beneath the sea would stay with him forever. Despite the evil purpose for which it was built, there was a grandeur about the concept and execution of the *Lepadus* that commanded respect. To see a mighty ship die was always sad, especially in a dense pall of black smoke and a sizzling, flame-scarred sea.

The Straits of Bonifacio were entered at dawn, and the *Wayne*, still underwater, veered to starboard. Bond sat in Carter's cabin wearing a wetsuit and checking his diving gear. The suit was a good fit. Tight enough to show the bulge of the Walther PPK in its oilskin bag against his left shoulder. Bond fitted the regulator to the neck of the scuba tank, tightened the wing nut that held it in place, and opened the air valve. He sucked a few breaths from the tank to make sure that it was feeding air and looked up to see Carter standing in the doorway.

"I think we're there. You'd better come up and take a look."

Bond picked up the tank, flippers, and mask and followed Carter to the control room. He gripped the handles of the periscope and looked toward the familiar snaggle-tooth outline of the rocky coast. Seen from a distance and the right angle, the jagged circular outline of the caldera was easily recognizable. Streaks of white surf showed at the entrance through the rocks. Bond shivered and turned the periscope to port. A small cove bit into the cliffs, and there was a suspicion of white sand. A steep climb and you would be on the lip of the caldera. He relinquished the periscope. "That's it. They've got an early warning device at the entrance to the harbor, so I'm going to make for the cove alongside. Can you take me in any closer? There's quite a current."

Carter looked at Bond's injured arm and shook his head. "If there was a medal for stupidity, I'd pin it on you right away."

Bond started to lift the tank and Carter stepped forward and held it so that he could slip his arms through the straps. "Remember what I said. An hour after you leave this vessel, I'm going to destroy Atlantis. You'll have to wait for the Italian Navy to take you off. I have strict orders not to surface. We don't want any reports of fishermen seeing submarines around at the time of the eruption."

Bond nodded and fastened the third strap around his waist. "Message received and understood, Captain. Where do you want me?"

Carter's jaw tightened. "I'm going to flood one of the missile tubes amidships. You'll be inside it. I'll open the outer door and you swim out. Will you be able to get enough lift with that equipment?"

Bond wasn't certain, but he nodded.

Fifteen minutes later, he stood hunched in the 21-inch firing tube reserved for a nuclear missile. It was an agonizingly tight fit, and the feeling of claustrophobia it induced exceeded anything that Bond had known. His face was pressed against the smooth circular tube, and his scuba tank scraped the wall behind him. It was dark and hot, and he felt like a man in a straitjacket. When the water started to pour in, he wanted to scream. Instead, he pulled his mask down, spat inside it, and with his elbows pressed against his chest rubbed the saliva over the mask. He settled it on his face and drew up the regulator tube, fitting the mouthpiece into his mouth.

He took a couple of breaths and felt the water rising above his waist. This was the moment of sheer death-knowing terror. The moment that the many men who had drowned with the rats on the *Lepadus* must have known. Supposing he couldn't move? Supposing he remained stuck in the tube and the regulator failed? The water passed over his face, less icy than the fear that surged with it. A stream of bubbles rushed up, and he tilted his head to see the hatch beginning to open. Three fathoms above his head there was morning light glinting down through the water. Now pause, fight the panic, flex the knees as far as possible. Push—but not too hard! Don't lose momentum against the side of the tube. Bond felt the scuba tank dragging against the metal and paddled wildly. For a couple of seconds he seemed locked, and then his stretching hands clawed against the top of the tube and he was able to pull himself from the chrysalis of death.

Like a basking whale, the three hundred feet of nuclear submarine stretched away on either side. Bond patted the hull as one might an obedient dog and began paddling toward the surface to make a sighting.

It took him ten minutes to reach the cove, and his arm was aching painfully as he raised his head behind the protection of an offshore rock. There was no one about. The merest hiss of surf on the virgin sand. Bond wanted to rest, but he knew there was no time. He had to drive himself forward. He came in close to the caldera and let the swell lift him onto an apron of pumice-stone rock made slippery by the passage of the sea and a coating of weed that rose and fell like the fur of an animal. He pulled himself ashore and tugged off his flippers, watching small striped fishes dart in and out with the passage of the swirling sea. The sun was still low but already adding some luster to the sinister gray of the wall that surrounded Stromberg's harbor.

Bond looked about him carefully and began to make his way up the loose shale of volcanic rock that ran away beneath his feet like whispers in church. It was like climbing up a pile of coke. He reached the lip and laid himself down with the mask and flippers beside him. He was breathing hard, and his shoulder throbbed. Below him was a narrow defile plunging down into the dark waters of the caldera. Two hundred yards away, the lab rose like a mixture of oil rig, and space-probe launching-pad. There was no sign of life. The helideck was empty. The *Riva* was not moored alongside.

Bond turned his eyes toward the shore. No vessels were moored against the ramp. The shutters on the buildings were closed. To all intents and purposes, Stromberg had abandoned his headquarters. But—Bond tried to analyze his presentiment rationally, but it was impossible. Something told him that Atlantis still contained life. He waited another minute, his keen eyes searching all corners of the caldera, and then crawled over the ridge and lowered himself into the defile. Now he was in shadow and the wetsuit chafed uncomfortably. He picked his way down, scraping knuckles and bare feet as he tried to use every inch of the protection that the crevasse offered. Within five minutes he was at the water's edge. He looked at his battered Rolex Perpetual; nearly half an hour had elapsed since he left the *Wayne*.

Quickly sluicing his mask in water, he pulled it over his head and began to don his flippers. Within seconds, he was sliding beneath the surface. To his irritation, he found that there was water inside the mask, so he let his feet sink and tilted his head back until he was looking up through the murky water. He pressed a hand against the faceplate and expelled air through his nose until the mask was clear. Now he drove forward, paddling hard with his feet, his arms straggling back along the length of his body. The only sound was of his breathing—a deep, hollow noise when he breathed in, a fluted thumping of bubbles as he exhaled. The sea was murky, close-textured, impenetrable to the eye. With every stroke of the legs, the tension mounted. Was some sonar device plotting his course through the water? Would a depth charge soon drift lazily down to rip the flesh from his bones? He pressed on, seeking to cure fear with movement. The journey seemed endless. Had he by chance veered to one side of his target? No, there it was in front of him, the inverted dome vaguely discernible through the murk.

He looked behind warily but there was nothing save a trail of bubbles. Conscious that these might be seen if he was too near the surface, he dived beneath the hull before making his way upward, brushing against the barnacle-encrusted side. The light grew in intensity and shoals of small fish veered sharply to one side like shimmering iron filings caught in the refraction of the sun. His head broke the surface, and he pushed his mask back and spat out the mouthpiece so that he could fill his lungs with sweet gulps of fresh air. There was no sound except that of water nudging the landing stage. He paddled toward it and pulled himself aboard, wincing at the pain in his arm. He could feel the escaping blood making the inside of the wetsuit slippery.

194

Unzipping the jerkin, he took out the Walther PPK. He then shed his diving gear, and without its cumbersome weight immediately felt better. He took several deep breaths and rose unsteadily to his feet. His respite on the *Wayne* had not been sufficient convalescence for the non-stop action of the last few days. He was drawing on his last resources of energy.

Moving his gear to the side of the pontoon, Bond began to ascend the stairway, pistol in hand. The catwalks and gantries which had once been lined with hard-eyed guards were now eerily empty. He came to the first stage and faced the elevator. Some internal voice spoke up urgently and told him not to use it. He moved to port and found a metal stairway curving up around one of the four tubular columns supporting the structure. He followed it warily and came to a point where two enclosed galleries parted at right angles. One was in shadow and the other half-exposed to the rising sun. The sea murmured thirty feet below, but there was a closer source of noise. From somewhere along the gallery that lay in shadow came the sound of voices.

Bond tensed and tried to pump new life into the pain-numbed fingers that were gripping the Walther. It was impossible to hear what the voices were saying, but they sounded agitated and were talking over each other as if trying to press home an argument. Bond moved forward from the stairway and began to creep along the gallery. Somewhere above his head was a persistent creaking noise like a shutter stirring in the breeze. He passed one door and could tell that the voices were coming from the next room. One of them was speaking urgent Italian. He ducked below a porthole and saw that the heavy metal door was ajar. Two steps and he threw his shoulder against it and burst inside.

The room was empty—empty save for two banks of television screens on opposite walls. They were all showing different pictures, and as Bond watched, he realized that they were commercial television programs being beamed from around the world. A quiz game from Tokyo, a situation comedy from New York, a news bulletin from

Rome. Bond pondered and arrived at the truth. This was where Stromberg must have waited to hear news of the end of the world. Horrified announcements and then, one by one, the screens going blank, the babble of voices dying away until there was complete and utter silence. The silence of the grave.

Bond shivered and was turning to leave the room when a voice stopped him dead in his tracks.

"Good day, Commander Bond. I have been expecting you."

Chapter 24

EXIT SIGMUND STROMBERG—
AGAIN

The voice was Stromberg's. It came, like the picture of him sitting in his vast armchair, from each of the screens in the room. The other images had been wiped away into oblivion. He appeared to be helping himself from a bowl of walnuts, cracking each one with slow, intense care.

Bond glanced at his watch. Less than fifteen minutes to Carter's deadline. There seemed little alternative but to play along with Stromberg. The thin, disembodied voice continued.

"I have been watching you for some time. Ever since you crawled from the sea, in fact." The voice became introspective. "An appropriate entrance in the circumstances. Did it occur to you, Commander Bond? Were you intending to rub salt in my wounds by enacting the role of some primordial creature bridging the gap between fish and man? I imagine not. Such foresight does not seem to be in your nature."

"I didn't come here for character analysis." Bond's voice was cutting. "Where's Major Amasova?"

Stromberg spread his hands wide. "Clearly not with me. Come, there are matters which I wish to discuss with you. She can be one of them. I am in Room 4C. Do not be alarmed. I am not armed." He slowly stretched out a hand toward a console. The screens went blank.

Stromberg dropped the nutcracker into the bowl and flicked a switch on the console. The two halves of the Romney portrait separated and revealed the screen of the TV monitor. Stromberg adjusted picture control and watched the evil grace of the great white shark careen through the water. A slight quickening of the pulse was revealed in the deepening red glow of his pupils. The socket mouth began to tremble in anticipation. The camera was covering the glass-fronted cavity of the death-trap of Room 4C, and Stromberg settled back in his chair and tightened his hands over the rounded arm-ends. He wanted to hear Bond scream as the girl had screamed. He wanted to hear the water rushing in, the gasps, the groans, the sounds of scrabbling, gasping, choking, mad-eyed panic. He wanted to see Bond torn apart while he was still alive. He wanted to watch until the images on the screen were obliterated by a thick, crimson curtain.

"Room 4C sounded a little dull. I preferred to talk to you face to face."

Stromberg spun around and found himself looking into the mean, glinting barrel of Bond's Walther PPK. Bond emerged from the shadows. "Now, let's return to my earlier question. Where's Anya?"

Stromberg raised a non-existent eyebrow. "Anya? Last time it was Major Amasova. Do I detect the signs of a developing and tender friendship?"

Bond moved the Walther six inches closer to Stromberg's heart. "We don't have time for small talk, Stromberg. In less than ten minutes, this place is going to be sunk by torpedo fire."

Stromberg spread his arms wide. "That is of no consequence, Commander Bond. I have already decided to die. My main interest is in ensuring that you die with me. I would have preferred that the shark got you, but that is a question of personal whim." Stromberg waved an arm towards the walls. "If you could see outside, you would be able to observe that we are sinking. Even a person of your limited intelligence and imagination must have wondered why I should place my laboratory here, Commander Bond. It is because she is a bathysphere and because the caldera is practically bottomless. When the volcano exploded, it gouged a socket descending over a mile into the earth. This is where I would have lain while the nuclear turbulence passed far overhead. Snug as a fetus in a womb. A womb which, but for you, would have given birth to a new and immeasurably better world!" Stromberg's voice ascended to a shriek. "But you destroyed that, and I will destroy you! As soon as you came aboard, I instigated the process which put this craft into a dive from which we will not recover. Slowly but inevitably we will descend until the pressure crumples this wasted structure like a tin can!"

Bond's mind quickly picked the meat from Stromberg's insane ranting. If they were sinking, what was Carter going to make of it? The answer came sooner than he anticipated.

A violent explosion lifted Bond's feet from the floor and the room tilted crazily. Carter had fired early, but who could blame him? He could not afford to let the prize escape. Bond was sprawled against the wall behind Stromberg's chair, the floor rising like a steep slope in front of him. He rolled aside as a chair hurtled toward him and searched for Stromberg and his gun. Six feet away, along the wall, Stromberg pounced greedily. The Walther PPK took shape in his hand and he steadied himself against the wall. The twin pinpoints of hate glinted triumphantly. Bond tensed for the feel of the first bullet burrowing into his flesh. The third small eye was trained unswervingly on his heart. And then the glass-and-steel table crashed down the room and drove against Stromberg's head like a battering ram. There was a sickening crunch, and the head elongated, pushing the eyes forward so that they bulged out like those of a fish. Even in death, thought Bond.

Another pile-driving explosion and an ominous groan of anguish from the smitten hull. The room slowly righted itself and a fast-moving stream of water entered the door and began to snake across the carpet as if searching for someone. Bond scrambled to his feet and prised Stromberg's fingers from his pistol. Although but recently dead, they were of a reptilian coldness.

Bond burst through the door shouting Anya's name. The water was now an angry tide tearing at his legs. He could see it frothing and bubbling as it welled up from a companionway farther along the corridor. A giant squid swirled past and then three angelfish. What the devil was happening? Then he realized. The aquarium! The tanks must have burst. My God, if Anya was down there! There would be no hope. He shouted again and struggled on against the current. The corridor divided and a metal rail ran along the roof. From it dangled the familiar roundel of an electromagnet, presumably used to move stores and heavy equipment.

Bond ducked past the cable and straightened up to find a shadow blocking his path. A shadow with the ominous substance of Jaws behind it. The great uneven head scraped the roof of the corridor. The lips divided in a chilling smile of welcome. The tree-trunk legs parted the current like the Colossus of Rhodes. Bond raised his gun to fire, but his lacerated arm was too slow. Jaws gripped his hand and dashed it against the wall shattering his knuckles like a row of peanut shells. Bond cried out in pain and drove his knee upward with all the force that desperation and anger could muster. Jaws grunted; spreading his hand over Bond's face he propelled him into the flood. Bond floundered backwards, scrabbling to find his feet. Next time it would be the teeth. Jaws was baring them, furling his lips back so that one could see into the disgusting black caverns of his nostrils.

Bond's aching limbs scraped metal and his despairing hand at last found something to cling to. He pulled himself from the flood and saw that he was hanging on to a small control box, attached to wires that led to the rail in the ceiling. Jaws lumbered on remorselessly, pacing each step against the increasing fury of the mounting tide. Now, the magnet dangled like a bait before the hideous metal teeth. The image set off a small explosion inside Bond's battered brain. Oblivious of the pain, he jabbed his shattered hand against the contact button on the control box.

The magnet sprang at Jaw's mouth and clung, whirring, to his teeth. He looked like some malformed baby sucking a large teat. Then a look of surprise spread over the gross features. A giant hand rose to pluck at the offensive object as if it was an impertinent fly. Bond pressed the second switch and the wire tightened and began to draw Jaws back against the current. Now both hands were tearing at the magnet, and Jaws twisted furiously like a fish on the hook. As Bond watched in fascinated horror, a relentless triangle streaked up behind the stricken giant. A huge, gray force launched itself through the wild water, and two rows of white teeth closed about the threshing flesh. Obscene sounds broke through the barrier of the imprisoned teeth and a wave of blood surged against Bond's chest. Like a man fleeing from a nightmare he turned and let the current carry him away from this mind-searing spectacle of hideous death. The image of the small red eye glowing with demonic purpose pursued him like an avenging fury.

"Anya!" Bond shouted to hear his voice and know that he was still alive. The current swirled him around a corner and turned into a whirlpool as it surged, white-tipped, against a wall of metal. Bond seized the rail of a companionway and dragged himself from the flood. The structure was listing at an angle of forty-five degrees and beginning to buckle. It groaned and shuddered as if in its death agonies. Ahead, a door twisted and sprang open with a metallic snap. A slim white hand appeared around it.

"Anya!" Bond launched himself forward, scrambling along the angle of deck and wall. Anya's head and shoulders appeared pulling themselves out into the corridor. Her eyes recognized him and then hardened as if frozen over with a layer of ice.

"Anya." He tried to reassure her with the sound of his voice. She must be in a state of shock. God knows what they had done to her. Then a pistol appeared in her hand.

The sight pointed toward the lopsided ceiling and then slowly swung down to cover Bond's heart. The finger started to tighten around the trigger.

"When this mission is over, Sergei will be avenged and you will be dead." The words came back to Bond with chilling clarity. He kept coming. "Anya, give me that gun." He stretched out his hand. The barrel began to waver. Bond closed his fingers about it and kept looking into Anya's eyes. She blinked as if awakening from a bad dream. The corridor echoed to the sound of grinding metal as if it had been twisted by two giant hands. Bond took the gun from the unresisting fingers and pressed Anya to his chest. He could feel her heart thudding like a bird's. "We have seconds to get out of this place. Trust me." He took her by the hand and drew her after him as a menacing column of water rushed between their feet.

Now the downward motion was terrifyingly perceptible. The stomach rose; the legs hung weightless. Bond's heart pumped blood and panic through his system. How in God's name did one escape from this waterlogged tomb? The walls were now listing at such an angle as to become a roof. Bond dropped to his knees and the water rushing past brushed against his chin. Soon it would be above his shoulders, his head—and then what? How many minutes of palsied dance before the body finally floated belly upwards, the legs and arms dangling down like those of some spent insect? Bond jerked his head above the rising torrent and held tight to Anya's hand. To port there was a bulkhead door, opening six inches above the tilting deck. Three inches from its bottom there was a small plaque. Two magic words were stencilled in four languages: ESCAPE HATCH.

Bond reached up and pulled the heavy metal lever. As the door fell open, it was necessary to plunge his head into the cavity to keep it above water. He dragged Anya after him and began to scramble into the narrow, padded spheroid. The water surged about his feet and battered against the tilted door, making it impossible to close. Anya joined him and together they leaned down into the raging torrent fighting to save their lives. The stricken craft twitched into its final descending spiral and in that instant, the door cleared the water. Bond's mangled arm drew it closed, and Anya threw the locking bolts. The wild flood thumped vengefully against the closure.

Bond gripped the lever and plunged it down. There was a grinding noise, a breakaway, a resentful tug—and then a sudden sense of floating in space. And then, most beautiful of all, a sensation of rising. A movement toward heaven like that of flowers drawn by the sun.

"James!"

Bond felt Anya's arms encircle him, and then he collapsed into unconsciousness.

Chapter 25

LOVE IN THE MORNING

Breakfast was Bond's favorite meal of the day.

And since he was supposed to be recuperating—hated word!—he determinedly made the most of it. Two large, strong cups of unsweetened black coffee. Half a pint of fresh orange juice—freshly squeezed with a couple of errant pips paying tribute to the immaculacy of the source. Two fried eggs and three thick slices of Irish bacon. When the slices were no more than three serpentine rinds he moved on to the toast. Two slices made more delectable by the addition of generous spreadings of Normandy *demi-sel* butter and Cooper's Vintage Oxford marmalade decanted into a silver pot that Bond vaguely remembered having been a christening gift.

Bond brushed a crumb from the corner of his mouth and was about to ring for May, his treasured Scottish housekeeper, when she appeared unannounced. "Excuse me, s." ('S' was May's grudging diminutive for 'sir'.) "There's a naval gentleman to see you. I think he's an American." The slight note of disapproval in May's voice did not totally exclude sympathy for the man's lot.

Bond felt better immediately. "Captain Carter?" he prompted—remembering names was not May's forte. "Ask him to come in straightaway."

Seconds later Carter strode in behind a strong handshake. His face crinkled up in a genuine smile of greeting. "Great to see you, James. I'm sorry to appear at this hour, but I'm on a tight schedule. I've got to call in at the Embassy, and then I'm flying back to the States. How are you?"

Bond extended his cigarette case to Carter, then slipped a Morlands between his own lips. "I'm here purely under false pretences—or perhaps impurely. I was cured days ago. I think my superiors must be trying to incarcerate me in my own home while they wonder what to do with me."

Carter's face became serious. "I wanted to express— hell! I mean, I wanted to say how wretched I felt about shoving those torpedoes up your backside. I saw the thing slipping away and—"

Bond held up a restraining hand. "I'd have done the same in your position—probably earlier. Anyhow, if you hadn't disobeyed orders and fished us out of the drink, I probably wouldn't be here now. When I was a child I was brought up to believe that it was the U.S. Cavalry that always arrived in the nick of time. Now I'm transferring my allegiance to the Navy."

Carter accepted Bond's outstretched hand and grasped it warmly. "Thanks. I hope we work together again sometime. Oh, by the way"—his eye twinkled—"there was some girl hanging around on the front doorstep when I arrived. I think she wants to see you."

"Do you think I'd want to see her?" asked Bond.

Carter pretended to consider the question and then nodded his head. "I think you might." He raised a hand to his temple and was gone.

Bond stood up, feeling a mounting sense of excitement spread through him. Was he being stupid? Could it be possible? Somebody came into the room behind him and he turned, expecting to see May.

It was Anya. She wore a black woolen coat down to her ankles and carried a large, soft leather grip. Her face

205

was as beautiful as he remembered it. Perhaps more so. The hair casually brushed back from the high cheekbones, the delicately tilted nose, the wide sweep of the sensual mouth. And, about her deep blue, richly lashed eyes, that wondrous quality of knowing innocence. She put down her bag and faced him squarely. "I have come to look after you."

Bond looked at her lovingly. "I don't need looking after. I'm perfectly fit. Right at this moment I feel better than I ever have done. Anyway, I have a housekeeper to look after me."

"The woman with the stern black uniform who was putting on her hat to go shopping when I arrived?" Bond smiled and nodded. "Does she hold a State Nursing Certificate, first class?"

Bond rested his hands on either side of Anya's slim shoulders. "Now you come to mention it, I rather think she does. Sweet, darling Anya. What are you doing here? What about Russia? What about your job?"

She looked up at him and her lips trembled. "Let us say I am on holiday. I will tell you all later—much later." She began to unbutton her coat.

"Right." Bond's nostrils flared. "I think you know the kind of treatment I need. I'm going to shave. When I come back, I'll expect to find you in bed."

He went into the bathroom and managed to shave without cutting himself. When he came back, Anya was in bed with a single sheet pulled up to her waist. Her slim, beautiful breasts curved toward him invitingly. Her long fingers rested on her thighs. She looked into his eyes unwaveringly. "James, you are not the first man that has made love to me."

Bond's hard, naked body moved toward the bed and his fingers closed around the sheet. "My darling," he said. "That remains to be seen." He came down on her like a hawk.

THE BEST OF BESTSELLERS
FROM WARNER BOOKS!

THE BEST OF BESTSELLERS
FROM WARNER BOOKS!